"I found out about **with."**

Kate hesitated, but eventually put her hand in Rafe's. "Where'd you hear about it?"

"Jake." He loved holding her hand. Used to do it all the time when he'd helped her out of his truck and when they'd danced at the Moose. All that had ended in August.

"So Millie told him and he called you?"

"It wasn't quite that straightforward." Once she was out of the truck, he let go of her. "This is Jake we're talking about. The point is, I know." He fought the urge to take her hand again. She steadied him, and he was about to make a commitment that made his chest feel like a war was being fought in there.

"All right. You know. Why are you here?"

His heart hammered. "Because I don't want you to work out a deal with some random guy who answers your ad."

"Too bad. I'm—"

"I'll do it, Kate." He cleared the huskiness from his throat. "I'll marry you."

STRONG-WILLED
COWBOY

THE BUCKSKIN BROTHERHOOD

Vicki Lewis Thompson

Ocean Dance Press

STRONG-WILLED COWBOY
© 2020 Vicki Lewis Thompson

ISBN: 978-1-946759-91-7

Ocean Dance Press LLC
PO Box 69901
Oro Valley, AZ 85737

This is a work of fiction. Any resemblance to actual persons, living or dead, business establishments, events, or locales is entirely coincidental.

Cover art by Lee Hyat Designs

Visit the author's website at
VickiLewisThompson.com

*Want more cowboys? Check out these other titles by
Vicki Lewis Thompson*

The Buckskin Brotherhood
Sweet-Talking Cowboy
Big-Hearted Cowboy
Baby-Daddy Cowboy
True-Blue Cowboy
Strong-Willed Cowboy

The McGavin Brothers
A Cowboy's Strength
A Cowboy's Honor
A Cowboy's Return
A Cowboy's Heart
A Cowboy's Courage
A Cowboy's Christmas
A Cowboy's Kiss
A Cowboy's Luck
A Cowboy's Charm
A Cowboy's Challenge
A Cowboy's Baby
A Cowboy's Holiday
A Cowboy's Choice
A Cowboy's Worth
A Cowboy's Destiny
A Cowboy's Secret
A Cowboy's Homecoming

1

"I like these." Rafe Banner leaned against the slanted back of an Adirondack chair and stretched his booted feet toward the warmth of the fire pit. October nights were chilly, which suited him. "Still don't know why we had to get eight, though. We only need seven."

"They were two-for-one." Leo drained the last of his hard cider.

"But we didn't have to take the eighth one because it was free."

"Doesn't hurt to have an extra."

"I'm with Leo on that." Garrett set his bottle on the ground beside his chair and got up to tend the fire. "Even with eight, we don't have enough on nights the women show up."

Rafe didn't comment. The subject of women was a touchy one for him now that he and Kate weren't getting along.

"Figured I'd find you jokers back here!" Nick came around the end of the bunkhouse and headed down the well-worn path. "What's this? Real chairs?"

"End of the season sale in Great Falls," Leo said. "Couldn't pass it up."

"I approve." Nick pulled one off the stack and put it next to Rafe's. "But why'd you get eight?"

Leo exchanged a look with Rafe. "Two-for-one."

"Did they make you take the eighth one?" He grabbed a bottle of cider out of the ice chest nearby.

"Of course not, but why wouldn't we?"

"Because we only need seven."

Rafe smiled at Leo. "See? I'm not the only one who thinks that way. When everybody's here, we'll have an empty chair."

"So what?"

"The group looks incomplete, like we're missing somebody."

"Exactly." Nick sat down and twisted off the bottle cap. "I like them, though. The seat fits my posterior."

"Glad you're pleased," Rafe said, "since we're billing you one-seventh of the cost."

"Fine with me." He sighed and gazed up at the stars. "Beautiful night." His tone oozed happiness.

Rafe was glad for him. He really was. "Good to see you, bro."

Nick grinned. "You just saw me this morning for barn duty."

"You know what I mean."

"Yeah, I do. It still feels a little strange, not living in the bunkhouse, but—"

"I take it Eva's hosting her friends tonight?"

"Yep." Nick sipped his drink. "I'd forgotten about it or I would've planned on having dinner with you guys."

"Did you eat?" Garrett was big on making sure everyone stayed fed.

"I did, thanks. Got a burger to go from the Moose and ate it while I drove. The ladies said I could stay, but girls' night is important to Eva. And hanging out here is important to me. It's all good."

"How's Fiona doing?" Leo might think he sounded casual, but he failed miserably.

Nick gazed at him. "She's fine. But she—"

"Never mind. Forget I asked." He lifted his bottle in Nick's direction. "Here's to the only one of us who made the bachelor auction work for him."

"I'll drink to that," Garrett said.

"Me, too." Rafe touched his bottle to Nick's. "You did good."

"I was damn lucky." He leaned back in his chair. "These are way better than our chummy stumps, but you can't leave them out all winter like those stumps. They'll be ruined. It's not like we have storage space in the bunkhouse, either."

"I thought we'd stack them on your bed," Leo said. "Since you won't be using it."

"Hey, it's not just me who's moved out. Pile them on Matt's bunk. Or Jake's. Or CJ's. Those guys won't be using theirs, either, unless they totally screw up."

"We probably should ask Henri about the extra beds," Rafe said. "Makes no sense to have eight of them and three wranglers using the space."

"I did ask her." Nick took another swig. "When I told her I was moving in with Eva, I mentioned all the empty bunks. She's not ready to reconfigure the setup. They're built-ins, for one thing."

Rafe glanced at him. "Did it sound like she might hire more hands? Because we don't need—"

"I didn't get that impression. Even if some of us aren't sleeping in the bunkhouse anymore, we still work for her."

Leo nodded. "She's not short-handed. Especially when we're heading into the winter season."

"Which means we can stack the chairs on the vacated bunks." Rafe glanced at Nick. "Including yours. Problem solved."

Nick frowned. "I'm not crazy about having you put heavy wooden chairs on my bunk."

"Rafe's pulling your leg," Leo said. "He wouldn't really—"

"Why not? Just pile all the unoccupied mattresses on one bed and put the chairs on the other four. It might look a little unusual, but—"

"It'll look terrible!" Leo sat forward. "I'm not living in a furniture warehouse, bro. We'll have to find—"

"Yeah, yeah, we'll figure out something else." Rafe grinned. "I wasn't serious. Although they'd be handy if we had a balmy day in January. We could haul 'em out, no problem."

"And the rest of the time the bunkhouse would look like a storage shed."

"We don't have to solve this tonight," Garrett said. "This weather's supposed to hold for another week or two."

"I hope so." Rafe gazed up at the clear sky. "The leaves have been amazing this year. They—" His phone pinged with a text. "'Scuse me a minute."

"If that's Henri, ask if she'd like to come on down," Leo said. "I'm in the mood for s'mores."

Rafe stared at his phone. "It's not Henri."

"Who?" Nick turned to him, his expression alert. Concerned. He had a sixth sense when it came to trouble brewing, especially for anyone in the Brotherhood.

"Kate. She wants to see me. Says it's urgent."

Nick met his gaze. "I thought you weren't talking."

"We're not."

"So what the hell?"

"Don't know." He stood. "Guess I'll go find out."

Technically he could have walked, but he hopped in his truck. It was about a three-minute drive from the bunkhouse to the three-bedroom cottage where Kate lived. Walking would have taken ten.

Her use of the word *urgent* made his stomach hollow out. She wouldn't have contacted him unless something was terribly wrong. Their last private conversation two months ago had been a disaster. He'd proposed. She'd said no. Definitely. They'd avoided each other ever since.

Adrenaline pumping through his veins, he parked next to her truck and climbed out. She'd lived alone since Millie, the housekeeper for the guest cabins, had moved in with Jake.

Would she have called him if Millie still lived here? When she'd been hired to cook for the ranch guests, she's moved into the cottage with Millie and they'd bonded. What if this urgent problem was an issue she and Millie would have handled together, like a flooded bathroom or a snake that had found its way inside the house?

Maybe he was working himself into a lather over a temporary emergency that could be quickly resolved. Except if she'd encountered that sort of situation, he'd be the last person she'd call.

His gut tightened as he took the steps two at a time and crossed the porch. "Kate! I'm here!"

She came to the door, her short curly hair golden in the glow from the porch light. An angel with a halo. A tired angel. There was no sparkle in her gray eyes.

He wanted what he'd always wanted, to wrap her in his arms and make her forget every bad thing that had ever happened to her. "What's wrong?"

She pushed open the screen door and stepped back so he could come in. "I have a huge favor to ask."

Music to his ears. "Anything. Name it." He took off his hat.

"Thanks for saying that. Considering." She gestured toward the living room. "Let's sit. Can I get you a drink? Something to eat?"

"No, thanks." Not a plumbing problem or a stray varmint, then. He left his hat on the little table by the door.

Walking into the achingly familiar living room, he chose the rocking chair so she could have the couch. That put the coffee table between them, which was just as well.

He hadn't been in this room or spent time alone with her since their horseback ride after the bachelor auction. First and only time he'd kissed her. This private moment made him want to do it again.

Clearly she wasn't in a romantic mood. She'd come straight here after finishing up at the dining hall. The damp spots on the sleeves of her blue plaid Western shirt told him she'd rushed through her cleanup routine.

She sat on the middle couch cushion, her back rigid, her denim-clad knees together, her boots aligned, her hands clasped tight. Something had her wrapped in barbed wire.

Taking a shaky breath, she looked at him. "My baby sister got accepted to Johns Hopkins University."

"Is that good?"

"It's one of the top medical schools in the country. Ginny's over the moon."

"Then good for her."

"It's also astronomically expensive. She doesn't have the money. Mom doesn't, either. And I'm still paying off the ginormous debt Enrique saddled me with."

"What's she going to do?"

"Apply for loans. Assuming she gets them, she'll go into debt. Crushing debt. Way worse than what I'm dealing with. She has no idea what that will feel like, carrying that burden, weighing it against every job offer, every missed opportunity. It will control her life, maybe for twenty or thirty years. But it's her only option so she's barreling ahead. It breaks my heart."

Her distress broke his. "I have a bank account, been saving a while, but from what you're saying, it wouldn't—"

"I'm not asking for money."

"What, then?"

"Have I ever told you about my Aunt Lilith?"

"Doesn't ring a bell."

"She's my mom's wealthy sister. Never had kids but her circle of friends all have at least one and they brag about them constantly. Aunt Lilith appropriated Ginny and me as surrogate kids she could brag about."

"Could she cover Ginny's expenses?"

"Easily. Ginny won't ask because she knows there'd be strings attached. She made Mom promise not to ask. I guess they assumed I wouldn't, either. But I did. And she agreed."

"With strings attached?"

"Oh, yeah. She hated my scandalous divorce, but she *really* hates that I won't repair my reputation by finding a new husband."

His chest tightened. He wasn't going to like what came next.

"She'll pay for Ginny's med school if I..." Her voice faltered. "Rafe, will you marry me?"

2

Rafe looked like he'd been sucker punched. The breath whooshed out of him and for a second, his brown eyes glazed over.

Shaking his head as if to clear it, he dragged in air. His gaze cleared. And sharpened. "You said favor. What's the catch?"

This was the hard part, but it had to be said. She didn't want any confusion. "It would be in name only, to satisfy Aunt Lilith until Ginny gets her degree."

He glanced away. "I see." His tone was quiet, too quiet.

"She'll graduate in four years."

He still wouldn't look at her. "Ginny's okay with this?"

"I think she will be if I frame it right. And I won't tell her until after the ceremony. That way it's a done deal."

"And how will you frame it?"

"I'll say we're good friends and we're just going through the motions to fool Aunt Lilith. It won't disrupt our lives at all."

He met her gaze. "It won't?" His tone was conversational but anger burned in his eyes.

"Why should it? You'd be free to do whatever you want."

"Would I, now?"

She flushed. "I mean, like date. I wouldn't expect you to—"

"Honor my vows?" His soft voice was at odds with his steely gaze.

She gulped. "I realize it's a lot to ask."

He broke eye contact and stood. "It's too much to ask." He headed for the door and grabbed his hat.

She started after him. "Would you at least think about—"

"No, Kate, I won't." He spun around, fury blazing in his eyes. "You rejected my offer of a real marriage." He hurled the words at her. "Now you want me to go along with a damned fake one! Find another sucker. I'm not available." Shoving the screen door open, he was across the porch and down the steps in seconds.

"Rafe!" She hurried across the porch. "You wouldn't have to live with me! You could—"

"Then anybody will do, right? Put an ad in the *Apple Grove Gazette*. You're a good cook. Offer to make the guy dinner once a week. That should be enough to satisfy the poor sap." Jerking open the door of his truck, he climbed in and slammed it shut. The engine roared to life and the tires spit gravel as he backed up and peeled out.

So much for that. God, she was tired. But she'd promised to call Millie after she'd talked with Rafe. Dragging herself back inside, she picked up her phone from the small table by the door and tapped it.

Millie answered on the first ring. "Well?"

"You were right. I probably explained it all wrong, but I doubt there was a right way. He's furious, offended, hurt, and thoroughly disgusted with me. I knew it was a long shot, but I thought if he understood the stakes for Ginny...."

"What are you going to do?"

"I don't know. It needs to be a valid marriage license and a legit ceremony. He told me anybody would do, but I'll be signing a legal contract. I can't just take somebody off the street."

"Certainly not. And if Rafe won't do it, neither will Leo or Garrett. They'd see it as disloyalty. Are you sure you can't talk your aunt into giving Ginny the money because it's the right thing to do?"

"If you knew her, you wouldn't ask that. She loves nothing better than exploiting a person's weakness to get what she wants. I'll pull this off. Somehow. If Rafe won't go for it, I'll find someone who will."

* * *

Kate didn't sleep much that night, and by morning she had a potential plan to run past Millie. She invited her over for mid-afternoon tea, a tradition they'd established when they'd lived together and had held onto even though Millie's living arrangements had changed.

Kate had made a convert of Millie, who'd had no interest in tea when they'd met. But a combination of delicate English teacups Kate had inherited from her English grandmother and loose, fragrant tea leaves had changed Millie's mind. A spoonful of local honey in each cup had sealed the deal.

Kate had the tea ready and a plate of brownies on the coffee table when Millie arrived, her bright red hair tied back with a pale green bandana. She claimed the rocking chair as usual, bringing it close enough to the table to put her feet up. Kate sat on the couch, her usual spot.

She hardly ever sat in the rocker and now she'd avoid it at all costs. It represented the moment she'd lost Rafe forever.

After stirring honey into her tea and putting a brownie on a small plate, she leaned against a couple of throw pillows she'd arranged for maximum comfort. No, that wouldn't work. She needed to be upright to present her plan effectively.

Millie sipped her honey-laced cinnamon tea. "Whatcha got?"

She picked up her phone and consulted the notes she'd made. "Rafe hit the ceiling, like I told you, but he gave me a couple of good ideas. I dismissed his comment about taking out an ad in the *Gazette*, but nearly everyone in town reads it."

"You're seriously planning to advertise?" She nibbled on her brownie.

"Why not? It's no different than listing any other job."

"I beg to differ. You're not looking for an employee."

"But I'm looking for someone to fill a position."

"A non-paying position."

"That's where Rafe's other idea comes in. He was being sarcastic, but it's not a bad idea. He suggested I offer to feed the guy dinner once a week in exchange for acting as my pseudo husband. I could do that on my night off."

Millie finished her brownie and reached for another one. "Here?"

"Why not?"

"It's too damned cozy. He's liable to get ideas."

"Which could get awkward."

"Unless it turns out you start liking the guy."

Kate made a face.

"It could happen."

"Nope. I'm never falling into that trap again. I had stars in my eyes when I married Enrique and glossed over the legal ramifications of becoming a man's wife. I'm still paying for that, literally. If I'm forced to do this to help Ginny, it'll be strictly business."

"If you say so. But I wish... I don't know what I wish, to be honest."

"It's probably a good thing Rafe turned me down. The idea of trying this with anybody else gives me the heebie-jeebies, though." She took a restorative breath. "But it's my only option, so let's keep brainstorming."

"Okay." Millie drained the last of her tea and set the cup and saucer on the coffee table.

"I still think offering to cook dinner for the guy might be a draw."

"I think so, too, but you don't have to eat with him."

"You're right. I could take it to his door and leave."

"Just don't offer to clean for him. That's too personal."

"And I don't enjoy it. Cooking is something I do like. And shopping for food. I wouldn't mind that, either. I'm a good bargain hunter. I could stretch his food budget so he'll eat better for less."

"You know, that might be enough for some guys. Find one who hates shopping and lives on frozen pizza."

"I could even provide a few frozen entrees he just has to heat up to get him through the rest of the week. If he's paying for the food, I'm only out the time to fix it."

Millie gazed at her. "Believe it or not, I can see this working. In exchange for going through a simple ceremony and signing a marriage license, a guy gets a personal chef for the next four years. He can date, hang out with friends, and likely get healthier."

"He can't get married."

"But he could have a really long engagement if he finds the perfect person. Your ad could say—Bachelors! Tired of frozen pizza every night? Want to eat better for less? I have the perfect deal for you!"

"I like it. I'll head down to the *Gazette* tomorrow. Tonight I'll tell Henri, because she should know. I doubt she'll have a problem with it since I won't let it interfere with my work."

"It'll take up a lot of your free time, though."

Kate shrugged. "Who needs free time? I don't party with you guys anymore, anyway."

"And we miss you."

"It's better for Rafe when I'm not there. The one time I went with everybody to the Moose, he was like a zombie. And he really hated it when I showed up for chuck wagon stew night."

"Then you need to hang out with us again, so he can get past that. If your plan works, you'll be busier, but surely you can fit us in here and there." She added an encouraging smile.

It wasn't enough to calm the butterflies. "You're right, I could, but..."

"But?"

She sighed. "It's not so easy for me, either. After last night, it'll be even more awkward."

"The more you show up, the easier it'll get. For both of you. And I'm not kidding about missing you. When you're not at our gatherings, they feel a little off. You're an important part of the gang, whether you know it or not."

Her throat tightened. "I know it. I'll do better from now on."

3

Rafe had just finished dinner cleanup duty in the bunkhouse kitchen when Jake texted. *Need help getting the desk I bought for the Raptors Rise Visitor Center out of my truck. You free?*

Be right there. He pocketed his phone and left the kitchen. Leo and Garrett had the checkerboard out and the potbellied stove going. The cookie jar sat on the table.

Leo glanced up. "Figured we could do a tournament. You in?"

"Sure, but Jake needs help unloading a desk for the visitor center. I should be back in fifteen, twenty minutes."

"Then we'll start and you can play the winner, which will be me."

Garrett laughed. "That's what you said last time."

"This time it'll be true. I can feel it."

"See you jokers in a few." Rafe unhooked his denim jacket from a peg on the wall and his hat from another one. "Don't eat all the cookies."

"No promises." Garrett set up his pieces on the wooden board. "Tell Jake the market was out of the chili powder he likes for chuck wagon stew. He needs to bring some from his house tomorrow night."

"Will do." Chuck wagon stew night was a weekly ritual he used to love, but he'd begun to dread it. When Kate had come after their fight, it had been torture. Then she'd stopped coming and he missed her like crazy.

He took the back road to the visitor center. Supervising the construction had been Jake's full-time job for the past couple of months and Rafe hadn't seen much of him.

Jake's suggestion to build a replica of a rustic log ranch house—porch, rocking chairs and all—was pure genius. The center looked as if it had been there forever. *Raptors Rise Sanctuary* was carved into a wooden sign hanging above the porch steps.

The lights were on and Jake's truck was backed up to the wide steps, the tailgate down. Rafe shut off the engine and climbed out to survey the situation. A massive desk sat in the truck bed, dollies underneath the carved legs at either end. Hauling that thing from Great Falls must have been tough on the shocks.

Jake walked out of the building and grinned. "Whatcha waiting for? I thought you'd have it out of there by now."

"I would have, but I didn't want to show you up." He gazed at the desk. "How much does that thing weigh?"

"You don't want to know. Once it's in the visitor center, it's not leaving."

"Where'd you get it?"

"Came out of an old bank building. I guess the president of the bank liked the idea of sitting behind it."

"Looks like you could dance on it and it wouldn't move."

"Once we get it in there, you can test that theory."

"Nah, I need to get back to a cutthroat checkers tournament in progress. Garrett said to tell you the market didn't have your chili powder and we're out. You need to bring some tomorrow night."

"Duly noted. Which reminds me of something. Kate has a plan for getting herself a husband and it'll probably work."

The dinner Rafe had just eaten threatened to come up. He swallowed hard. "None of my business."

"Maybe not, but you're the one who gave her the idea."

"The hell I did."

"Millie talked to her this afternoon. Tomorrow she's putting an ad in the *Apple Grove Gazette*."

"And you believe that? She just said it knowing it would get back to me."

"I wouldn't be so sure. She and Millie nailed down the wording during their tea break. It's aimed at single guys who either hate to cook or don't know how."

"*Damn it.*" He began to pace. "I did give her that idea but I never thought—" He spun toward Jake. "Is she gonna put in the husband part?"

"No. That'll be discussed during the personal interview."

Personal interview? Any minute his head would explode. "Where's she planning to do that?"

"At Gertie's."

Panic messed with his breathing. "If she strikes a deal, would he come to the house for meals? I can't believe she'd—"

"It's more elegant than that. She'll handle his food budget, shop for him and deliver several home-cooked meals a week—one hot and the rest frozen and ready to heat up."

"That's a terrible idea. She doesn't have time for that nonsense."

"Of course she does. She's efficient. It'll eat up most of her spare hours, but it's doable. I can already think of half-a-dozen guys who would take that setup in a heartbeat."

He could, too. "I can't let her do this."

"I knew you wouldn't like it, but—"

"I *hate* it. She'll run herself ragged shopping and preparing nice meals for some idiot, when all he has to do in return is stand up with her and sign a piece of paper."

"And spend four years legally married to her, which means if he falls in love with someone else, he's—"

"What if he falls in love with *her*?"

Jake gazed at him, his expression infuriatingly calm. "I suppose that's always a possibility."

"You *know* it is, bro. A *very* good possibility. She's beautiful, funny, and an amazing cook, which he'll figure out real fast once he starts eating what she brings. What guy wouldn't fall for someone like that?"

"You tell me."

"I can't let her go through with it."

"So you said."

He blew out a breath. "Let's get this desk inside. I have things to do."

"You don't have to move it."

"Hey, I said I'd help you and I—"

"Matt's on standby, waiting for my call. You're free to go see Kate."

"Who said I was going to see Kate?"

"You're not?"

"Okay, I am, but what do you mean, Matt's on standby?" The light dawned. "You got me over here so you could tell me about the ad."

"Yep. Found out about it during dinner with Millie. Matt was planning to help me until I told him to hold off and let me ask you, first."

"You didn't have to make it so complicated. You could have explained it to me over the phone."

Jake grinned. "Yeah, but this was more fun. Now get the hell out of here."

Rafe started toward his truck. Then he turned back. "Thanks, bro."

Jake looked up from his phone. "Don't mention it."

"And thank Millie for me."

"I will. Now go."

"Right." Rafe lengthened his stride and was in his truck with the motor going in no time. Picking up his phone, he called Leo and tucked the phone into its holder on the dash.

"Hey, Rafe, you're late."

"I'm headed over to Kate's." He backed around and pulled away from the visitor center.

"I thought you never wanted to set foot in that house again."

"Things changed. I'll give you an update when I get back. I won't be long."

"Stay as late as you want, but don't expect cookies when you get here."

"Just so there's hard cider in the fridge."

"Always. Good luck, bro."

"Thanks." He disconnected the call and checked the time. She might not be home from the dining hall yet. Hadn't figured on that, but it didn't matter. He'd wait.

Sure enough, her truck wasn't parked in front of the cottage and no lights were on inside. He shut off the motor, got out and leaned against the fender.

The scent of burning cedar drifted from Henri's house, but smoke wasn't coming from the chimney. Paper lanterns glowed in the backyard and Ben's truck sat in the front. She must be using the cast-iron fire pit Ben had given her.

Ben had been spending less time at the Moose and more evenings at Henri's. Looked like a courtship was in progress. Was a wedding in their future? Henri wasn't talking.

Rafe returned his attention to the cottage. So peaceful. Had it only been twenty-four hours since he'd barreled out of there, filled with rage?

Driving around for an hour after leaving her house had helped some. Talking it through with Leo and Garrett had helped some more. He'd had a heart-to-heart with Nick while they'd mucked out stalls this morning.

But despite their understanding and support, his anger had stuck with him, simmering under the surface. Then Jake had revealed Kate's self-sacrificing plan and the anger had drained away.

He'd underestimated the depth of her commitment. He shouldn't have. Going to the mat for her baby sister was totally in character.

At the sound of a truck engine, he pushed away from the fender and stood. Headlight beams swept the parking area as she pulled in. She slowed the truck, creeping forward as if buying time to compose herself.

He hated that his unexpected appearance caused that reaction. She used to greet his surprise visits with a happy smile. They used to be friends.

Walking to her truck, he opened her door. "Don't be scared. I'm not mad anymore."

"That's not what I heard from various sources today."

He swung the door wider and offered his hand. "That was before I found out about the idea you'd come up with."

She hesitated, but eventually put her hand in his. "Where'd you hear about it?"

"Jake." He loved holding her hand. Used to do it all the time when he'd helped her out of his truck and when they'd danced at the Moose. All that had ended in August.

"So Millie told him and he called you?"

"It wasn't quite that straightforward." Once she was out of the truck, he let go of her. "This is Jake we're talking about. The point is, I know." He fought the urge to take her hand again. She steadied him, and he was about to make a commitment that made his chest feel like a war was being fought in there.

"All right. You know. Why are you here?"

His heart hammered. "Because I don't want you to work out a deal with some random guy who answers your ad."

"Too bad. I'm—"

"I'll do it, Kate." He cleared the huskiness from his throat. "I'll marry you."

4

Be careful what you wish for. Kate gulped. She'd adjusted to the new plan and had convinced herself it was better than her original idea of asking Rafe. Being legally bound to a relative stranger who would be compensated for his trouble was a more impersonal setup.

She glanced at Rafe. The darkness combined with the shadow of his hat kept her from getting a good view of his face. "You were justified in being upset with me. I'm not sure I trust this change of heart."

"You wounded my pride. I thought you had a lot of nerve, asking me."

"Which is a legitimate reaction. You have every right to—"

"But when Jake told me what you're willing to put yourself through to help Ginny, I was ashamed of myself. You shouldn't have to go to some stranger to get the help you need. You should get that support here. And I'm the logical person to give it."

"I thought that way in the beginning, but now I realize you're right. It's too much to ask. A marriage arranged for financial reasons would stick in your craw."

"I can handle it."

"Can you? You may be the tallest, brawniest cowboy at the Buckskin, but you're a sentimental sap. Don't bother denying it, because I know it's true."

"I'll just keep in mind why we're doing it. This isn't about me. It isn't about you. It's for Ginny."

"That's very noble, but I can't let you participate in a mockery of something you believe in. I should have considered that more carefully before I asked you to—"

"It *will* be a mockery if you stand up with somebody you barely know. But if you're with me, we can think of it as pledging our friendship. And by the way, I'd like to rebuild that. The current situation sucks."

"It does." She took a deep breath. "We can work on the friendship issue, but my new plan is the way to go. I don't want you involved. It's not fair to you and I should have realized that in the first place."

"Damn it, Kate, the idea of you ferrying cartons of food over to some undeserving—"

"He won't be undeserving. He's giving up the right to get married to someone else for the next four years. That's a huge restriction."

"Not for me."

"How can you say that? You want a wife and kids. Postponing that option for years means postponing your dream. Maybe I'll find somebody younger who—"

"Now we're talking about some wet-behind-the-ears kid? Good Lord."

"Not a kid, but maybe someone in his mid-twenties who's not ready to settle down."

"And horny."

"What?"

"You didn't think of that? Okay, you're not a guy, so you don't get it, but it'll be a turn-on to have a great-looking woman show up with delicious food she's cooked with her own two hands."

"Plus a stove and a few pots and pans." She liked the *great-looking woman* part, though.

"He won't see the hard work you've put into it. The food appears by magic. I know what it's like to be twenty-five. If he doesn't make a pass, I'll eat my hat."

"So what if he does? I'm not some blushing virgin. I can deal with that if it happens."

"There's no *if* about it. It will happen. Look, let's just simplify this. We'll have a quick, no-nonsense ceremony and call it good. Life returns to normal and you won't have to worry about delivering food to a randy twenty-five-year-old."

"You'll hate going through the ceremony."

"No, I won't. And we'll throw a party after it's over. Out by the fire pit. Leo and Garrett picked up some awesome Adirondack chairs on sale."

"No more chummy stumps?"

"You can use them as footstools. What do you say? Can we keep this issue in the family?"

"Oh, Rafe, I don't know. You and I have such a complicated—"

"It has been. I'll give you that. But everything's out in the open, now. The gang will know why we're staging this wedding. They'll be in on it. We're putting one over on your Aunt Lilith so Ginny's dream will come true."

"I'll admit it's more appealing than my concept. Mine has major dreariness potential. You're saying we'll tell everybody? The Babes, too?"

"My guess is they already know you asked me for help and I stormed out like a three-year-old throwing a tantrum. If we announce we've mended fences so we can pull off a decent wedding to fool your aunt, that will give me back some lost points."

She couldn't help smiling. "So it *is* about you."

"In that sense, yes. I'm not proud of how I reacted to your request. I want a do-over so I can prove I'm a better man than that."

Her heart swelled. She didn't know a better man than Rafe. "Then I guess we'd better get married."

"Excellent." His chest heaved. "I'm off for a couple of hours tomorrow afternoon. We can drive over to Choteau and get the license during your afternoon break."

"Never mind. I'll handle everything. You don't have to—"

"Might as well get the license together. Gather up all our paperwork. I can get you a list of what you'll need."

"Okay. I guess that makes sense. Is two o'clock good for you?"

He nodded. "Perfect."

"Is there a waiting period? I haven't checked into any of this."

"No waiting period."

"How do you know?"

"Let's just say I prepared for something that didn't work out. If we get right on this, we can get married on Saturday."

She blinked. "This Saturday?"

"Wait. You're scheduled to work. Would Sunday be better, since you're off?"

"I guess it would. Wow, this weekend, then. That's fast."

"The sooner you produce a husband, the sooner Ginny gets her money, right?"

"Good point. That's a definite advantage of going this route. With both of us planning it, we'll have it organized in no time."

"Not to mention the magic that happens when you call in the troops. One of us should contact Henri and—"

"Oh, no, Henri! She's expecting me. I asked if I could come and see her right after work. I wanted to lay out my new idea."

"We could go see her now."

She glanced up the hill. "Aw, look at that. She and Ben must be enjoying the new fire pit."

"Think you should text her before we tromp up there?"

She laughed and pulled out her phone. "Might not be a bad idea."

"God, I love that sound."

"What sound?" She composed a quick text to Henri and sent it off.

"You laughing." His voice was gruff with emotion. "Haven't heard it in a while."

She glanced up, her throat tight. "Are you sure about this? You can still back out. It's one thing to talk about it, but I'm still worried that when the time comes, you'll...."

"Lose it?"

"Yes." *And that would break my heart.*

"I won't. I promise."

Her phone pinged. After glancing at it, she took a shaky breath. "Then let's go tell Henri and Ben. They're waiting for us."

5

After ten years of working with Henri, Rafe could read his boss and stand-in mom pretty well. She didn't believe he could pull off this wedding. That little crease between her brows was a dead giveaway.

But she didn't say so. If she thought he was insane and headed for disaster, she'd tell him privately. Ben didn't look totally convinced, either. Rafe would just have to make believers out of them this weekend.

"So." Henri, seated cozily next to Ben in matching lawn chairs, leaned forward. "You'll have a brief ceremony, which you'll arrange, and a limited guest list, which I'll handle from the names we just discussed. Have you chosen a venue?"

"If you'd be willing," Kate said, "right here would be perfect." She glanced at Rafe. "Unless you're thinking of something—"

"I'd like to have the ceremony here if Henri's okay with it on short notice."

"Of course I am. Millie and I will put our heads together and come up with some tasteful decorations."

"I'll help with that," Ben said. "We have the decorations from Matt and Lucy's reception."

"Thank you." Kate looked relieved. "I realize that's extra trouble, but we'll need authentic looking pictures to convince Aunt Lilith the wedding is real."

"I'll ask Ed to take those," Henri said. "And video. She'll put together a digital montage that you can send straight to your aunt's inbox. It'll knock her socks off."

"That sounds wonderful. Is there something I can do for Ed? I'd bake her something, but since she has a live-in cook, that makes no sense."

"Invite her for afternoon tea sometime and serve it with your grandmother's china. She's dived into genealogy and it turns out her ancestors are from England. She's all about tea and old cups, now."

"Then I'll do that. Great idea."

"Speaking of receptions," Rafe said, "Kate and I would like to have ours out at the fire pit behind the bunkhouse." Damn, that sounded exactly like a bridegroom talking. *In name only, dude.* His chest tightened.

Henri nodded. "I like that plan. Listen, are you sure you want to do this on Sunday? Saturday feels more celebratory."

"Sunday's fine," Kate said. "I don't want to disrupt things any more than we have to. We can make Sunday work."

"I'm sure you can, but I'd like to ask Gloria to cover the whole weekend so you can switch the event to Saturday."

"Only if you'll dock it from my vacation time."

"We can talk about that later."

Rafe smiled. That was Henri-speak for *nice try, but I'm not doing that.*

"I'll take you off the Sunday work schedule, too, Rafe. Then you both can party all you want on Saturday night."

"That's generous." He glanced at Kate. "Are you okay with switching to Saturday, then?"

Her expression was hard to read. "Seems like a better choice."

"Good." Henri gave a quick smile of satisfaction. "You two can relax on Sunday, catch your breath."

Together? Nope. Saturday night he'd go back to the bunkhouse like always and she'd head home to the cottage. If he wanted to see her on Sunday, he'd have to create a reason.

Maybe she'd like to head into town, see a movie in the afternoon and grab a bite at the Moose for dinner. Or not. They'd never done that sort of thing by themselves, only with the gang.

"Do you have a dress, Kate?"

Henri's question redirected his attention. He'd need something special to wear, too. Didn't own anything that qualified.

"Not exactly. I have the one I wore for Lucy and Matt's wedding, but I'd rather not—"

"I agree. It's clearly a bridesmaid's dress. But we don't have much time."

"Rafe and I are going to get the license in the afternoon."

"Would you let me take you shopping in Great Falls after breakfast tomorrow?"

"Would we have time? I need to be back to serve lunch in the dining hall."

"Unless I put Garrett in charge of lunch for the guests. Would you be comfortable with turning the dining hall kitchen over to him?"

"Of course. But it's my job, so I should—"

"Unusual circumstances call for flexible plans. Let's do that. I know just the shop we'll go to. When are you guys going to the courthouse?"

"We'd planned on leaving at two," Rafe said, "but it could be a little later than that."

"Two is doable."

"Just so I know what to expect..." Kate looked uncomfortable. "What's the price range at that shop?"

Henri's expression softened. "I was planning to treat you."

"That's a very sweet offer, but I can't accept. You're already doing so much, considering we're springing this on you at the last minute."

"Here's the thing. Your Aunt Lilith makes my blood boil and it would calm me considerably to see you two looking amazing in the pictures you send her. While I suspect Rafe has enough squirreled away to rent an appropriate outfit, I doubt you can afford the sort of dress I have in mind. Please let me get it for you."

Ben chuckled. "Run up the white flag, Kate. When Henri takes that tone, it's best to just go along."

"Okay, I will." Kate faced her. "I want to look amazing, too, and you're right about my budget. But I'll be delivering brownies to your doorstep for the next year."

"And I'll gladly accept them. Then that's settled. One more detail. Are you going to have anyone stand up with you?"

"Oh! I didn't think of that. Rafe? Should we?"

"I guess so, but... maybe just a best man and maid of honor."

"That works," Henri said. "It's a small, intimate wedding, so a best man and maid of honor are plenty."

"Then I'll ask Nick."

"And I'll ask Millie. She could wear her dress from Matt and Lucy's wedding. She looks fabulous in that pale green."

"I'll need to contact the tux rental place in Great Falls in the morning." Rafe's head was spinning. Should he have suggested next weekend, instead? No. The sooner this was over with, the better... for everyone.

"Since Kate and I will be in Great Falls, anyway, let us take care of the tuxes for you and Nick. I'll bet they could pull up the data from Lucy and Matt's wedding. If you're okay with what you wore then, we could bring it back with us."

"That would be great." He reached in his hip pocket. "Let me give you some—"

"We can settle up later."

"Okay." She'd try to pay for those outfits, too, but he wouldn't let her. This wasn't the time to hash it out, though.

Henri glanced at Kate. "Do you want someone to walk you down the aisle?"

She hesitated. "I suppose I could just go by myself."

"If that's what you want. But if you'd like me to—"

"Oh, yes, please! That would be so special, if you wouldn't mind."

Henri's gaze was tender. "I'd be honored."

"So would I." She took a shaky breath.

She had to be as bush-whacked as he was. He caught Henri's eye. "How about we leave the rest of the details for tomorrow?"

"Sure thing." Her expression filled with sympathy. "There's not much more. We've covered the main points."

Kate stood, which prompted everyone else to do the same. "I don't know how to thank you, Henri."

"Hey, that's what families are for."

"That's what Rafe said." She sent him a look of gratitude. "I haven't been here as many years as he has, and I suppose I didn't quite get it." Her voice trembled as she faced Henri. "Now I do."

"Aw, sweetheart." Henri gave her a hug. "I'm glad we could be here for you."

"M-me, too. And we'd better head home. Tomorrow will be a busy day."

"Yeah, let's vamoose." Rafe met Henri's gaze as he touched two fingers to the brim of his hat. "Thank you."

She smiled, although the tiny crease between her eyebrows remained. "Anytime."

Turning, he followed Kate down the hill and caught up with her in a couple of strides. "Are you okay?"

She nodded. "It's a lot to take in."

"Yes, ma'am."

"I'm going to call Millie tonight."

"Thought I'd call Nick, too. When will you notify your aunt?"

"I can take a picture of the marriage license tomorrow and text that. I'll let her know the ceremony is Saturday and I'll email pictures to confirm it. I want the money to start flowing to Ginny ASAP."

"When are you going to tell Ginny and your mom about the wedding?" He walked with her past the trucks and kept on going. Might as well see her to her door.

"I'll call Sunday. I'll tell them how much fun we all had outwitting Aunt Lilith. And that we can't wait for Ginny to start living her dream."

Regret tightened a fist around his heart. "I'm sorry I acted like a louse when you first asked."

"You acted like what you were—a wounded bear." She reached the door and turned to face him. "No more recriminations, Rafe."

The porch light created the halo effect again in her short blond curls and her eyes had turned a soft gray, which they did whenever she was over-tired.

He'd let her down yesterday. Not one of his finer moments. "I just wish I'd—"

"I mean it. You're about to do me a favor I can never repay."

"I don't get brownies?"

"As many batches as you want, for as long as you want, but there aren't enough brownies in the world to equal the sacrifice you're making for me."

"Now who's into recriminations?"

She sighed. "You're right, but I—"

"Kate, I'm doing this because I want to. I'll admit it's a freaky situation, but we'll handle it."

Her jaw firmed. "Yes, we will."

"I have a question about your mom and Ginny, though. Clearly you have no intention of having them at the wedding."

"There's no reason. When I explain why we did this, they'll understand why I didn't include them. They don't have money for a flight and it's a two-day drive to Apple Grove."

"Will they come out eventually?"

"Probably, when they can work it out, so they can express their gratitude to you. It'll be fine, though."

"Okay." It would be weird as hell, but no reason to debate something that would be far in the future. "Guess I'd better let you go in so you can call Millie."

"Right." She didn't move. "I just need to say something."

"No more recriminations, remember?"

"I remember." She squared her shoulders and lifted her chin. "I admire the hell out of you for stepping up to do this. I'll never forget that you came through for me in the clutch." Her voice softened. "You're awesome, Rafe Banner."

He sucked in a breath and clenched his jaw against the response he wanted to make. He'd told her two months ago what was in his heart. No point in repeating it now. "Thank you." He tipped his hat. "Have a good night."

On the drive home, he almost called Nick. Changed his mind. That call would go better if he had a cold bottle of cider in his hand. Leo and Garrett might have turned in by now. No problem. A little peace and quiet would be—

Holy hell. He stared at the row of pickups in front of the bunkhouse. He barely had room for his. And he'd never been so happy about that. The Brotherhood had gathered. For him.

6

Kate convinced Henri to let her buy lunch since it was an inexpensive fast-food option. They ordered their sandwiches and drinks to go and had their meal in the truck on the drive home.

"I love that dress on you." Henri was an expert at eating and driving, clearly a veteran of road trips to Great Falls that involved consuming food on the way back. "The silver threads in the fabric look so great with your blond hair and your gray eyes."

"If you ask me, they used sterling silver threads. I've never owned a piece of clothing this pricey."

"The way I figure, if you need to do something tough, you might as well do it in style. You look like royalty in that dress. And the vest we added to Rafe's tux will go great with it."

"I wonder how he'll feel about silver brocade. He's such a down-to-earth guy."

"He won't even notice."

"How could he not notice? He'll be wearing it."

"He'll be so keyed up over this ceremony that we could give him a purple spandex work-out suit and he'd put it on."

"He probably would, poor guy. We talked last night about ditching the recriminations, but I still feel guilty. Ginny is my baby sister and I'd do anything for her, but he has no such allegiance."

"Only to you."

"Am I trading on that right now?"

"No. When he turned you down, you came up with an alternative. He talked you out of it, so this is on him."

"You know about my plan to put an ad in the paper?"

"Everybody knows. When Rafe walked into the bunkhouse last night, the entire Brotherhood was there. Matt and Jake put out the call. All was revealed. Much cider was consumed. I heard about it first thing this morning."

Relief flooded through her. "I love them for doing that for him. Makes me feel a hundred percent better to know they're giving him moral support."

"You have their support, too."

"I do? Even if I'm the source of the—"

"As I said, he's a grown man with the right to make his own decisions. Nobody's holding a gun to his head. If he didn't want to do this, he could have let you go ahead with your Plan B."

"Yeah, he really hated that idea."

"I'm not surprised." Henri set her drink in the cup holder. "Okay, let's take stock. We have the clothes. Ed's bringing folding chairs and an arched trellis. We're using whatever fall decorations Millie has and whatever Ben has stored at the Moose. Garrett and Jake have the food under control for the reception around the fire pit. Have you gathered up what you need to take to the courthouse?"

"I have. Rafe texted me a list this morning."

"What about flowers?"

"*Flowers.* That's like a wedding staple, isn't it?"

"I think so. Aunt Lilith will expect it. Do you have a favorite kind? Ed's poised and ready to have them flown in."

"No, no, we're not flying in anything. What's in the flower aisle of the market right now? You'd think I'd know, but when I shop there, I skip that section completely. I don't have a favorite. Let's go with something pretty and available."

"That's mums, and I have some growing in my yard. I have more than enough."

"Perfect! I vote mums for me, mums for Millie, and mums for any other situation that needs a touch of color."

"Lucy's an artist. Let's ask her to create a bridal bouquet and one for the maid of honor. If she has time, she could do something with the arched trellis—maybe autumn leaves and mums."

"Sounds great to me. Should I call her or would you like to?"

"I nominate you. I have a sandwich, a drink and I'm driving. Last I checked, you just had a sandwich."

"I'm on it." She called Lucy, who was eager to help with the flowers. Kate hung up and turned to Henri. "Everyone's being so nice about this crazy scheme."

"Nobody likes a bully."

"Aunt Lilith?"

"Yes, Aunt Lilith. It's hard to believe you came from the same family tree. Why do you think she's so nasty?"

"My mom says it's partly because Aunt Lilith's the second-born and she's always been unhappy about it. But their biggest fight was over my dad. They both liked him and he chose my mom."

"Probably because your mom's nice and Lilith's a pain in the ass. I'm just sorry he died so young."

"It hasn't been a bed of roses, but Mom's a survivor."

"How did Lilith end up in the chips?"

"She married a very rich older man. Then he conveniently died, leaving her with piles of money."

"Well, I'm all for prying her away from some of her precious money. Oh! I just thought of one more thing. Do you have someone in mind for conducting the ceremony?"

"Yikes! That would be an important detail, wouldn't it?"

"It would, especially at the last minute."

"How well do you know the pastor at the Apple Grove Church?"

"Not well. He's new, and I haven't gone much since Charley died."

"When I married Enrique, the pastor insisted on several counseling sessions. Would this guy want that?"

"I think he did something similar with Matt and Lucy, now that you mention it."

"I'll try to find his contact info. Ah, here we go." She keyed in the number. After a couple of rings, his voicemail clicked on.

This is Reverend George Stevens. Sorry I missed your call. I'm currently attending a retreat and will be unavailable until late Saturday night. See you in church on Sunday!

Kate disconnected the call. "That's clearly not an option."

"I just remembered something."

"You're an ordained minister?"

"You don't have to be to marry people in Montana. Or in most states these days."

"I didn't know that. In any case, I thought you were walking me down the aisle."

"I am. I wasn't thinking of me. Red used to perform marriage ceremonies."

"Red? Anastasia?"

"Yep. She's gone into semi-retirement to concentrate on her barrel racing and jewelry, but if you don't mind a little kookiness in your ceremony, I'll bet she'd do it if you ask."

"And it's legal? I don't want Aunt Lilith challenging this."

"It's absolutely legal. Getting the marriage license is the legal part. The ceremony is just the icing on the wedding cake."

"Oh, my God, that's something else. A cake. I'll bet if we don't have a picture of us cutting a big ol' cake, Aunt Lilith will—"

"I was going to surprise you with this, but I guess you need to know. Ed's chef is making a cake. The Babes will take care of getting it out to the fire pit."

Kate's throat tightened. "That's..." She had to clear her throat and start again. "That's so...." She couldn't go on.

Henri gave her a quick glance. "It's okay, I hope? That I didn't consult with you about the cake?"

She nodded vigorously and thumbed tears from her eyes.

"Did I make you cry?"

She gulped. "Happy tears."

"Well, those are just fine." Henri reached over and patted her arm.

Kate took several deep breaths and leaned back against the seat. "Bless the Babes."

"I've said that more times than you can imagine. Hey, look at that, we're home already. And look who's waiting to take you to the Teton County Courthouse."

7

Rafe levered himself out of the Adirondack chair on Kate's porch as Henri drove in. Nice of her to drop Kate off here before heading up to her house. Typical Henri, though. She was pulling out all the stops for this wedding.

He clattered down the steps and made it to the passenger side of the truck in time to open Kate's door.

She picked up a sack of trash from one of the fast food chains in Great Falls before she let him help her down. "How long have you been waiting?"

"Not long. I'm early, but I'd finished my work and decided to come on over in case you got back sooner."

"And here we are." She closed the door. "If you'll grab the stuff in the back seat, I'll run in and get my paperwork."

"You bet."

"Hey, Rafe," Henri called from the driver's seat. "I heard about last night's party. How're you doing after all that booze?"

"Just fine, ma'am. Thanks for asking." He opened the back door.

"The garment bag is for you and Nick. They had your sizes in the computer, just like I thought. I told them to hang onto the file, since we'll likely have more weddings in the future."

"Good idea." He lifted the garment bag from the hook above the door frame. Draping it over one shoulder, he grabbed the large, elegant shopping bag in his other hand. "I sure do appreciate this. What do I owe you?"

"We'll talk about it later."

He laughed. "We're not playing that game. You can't cover the cost of the entire wedding. How much?"

"Tell you what. You pay Red the honorarium for performing the ceremony and we'll call it even."

"Red? I thought she quit doing that."

"She's agreed to step in, since the pastor of the church isn't available tomorrow."

"That's very sweet of her. And I'll happily pay her going rate, but the honorarium would be my expense to begin with, so I still—"

"It's almost two." Henri put the truck in reverse. "You'd better take that stuff in the house so you can head out. No telling how many other couples are ahead of you."

"Good point, but don't think I'm letting this go."

"We'll discuss it when things calm down."

"All right. And thank you for taking Kate shopping." He held up the bag. "Looks like you found something."

"Oh, we did, and you'll love it, but you're not allowed to see it until the ceremony."

"Henri... this isn't...."

"I know. Not a wedding in the sense most people think of it. But—"

"Nothing will change. It's just a piece of paper."

"But without that piece of paper, the rest is pointless. Better get truckin', cowboy."

"Yes, ma'am." He closed the door and gave her a wave.

She backed her truck around and drove toward her house. He started toward the cottage.

Just a piece of paper. He'd been telling himself that ever since he'd opened his eyes this morning, his brain fuzzy from drinking with the Brotherhood.

But the trip to the courthouse brought everything into sharp focus. It was as real as the earth beneath his boots and the blue autumn sky overhead. This afternoon he was getting a license to marry Kate.

She was standing on the other side of the screen door as he started up the steps. "I waited in here, in case you had anything private to discuss with Henri."

"Nothing private, just the usual." He opened the door and she stepped aside as he walked in. "She wants to pay for Nick's and my duds and I'm not letting her do that."

"Good luck getting her to take the money. I figured you'd want to leave the garment bag in the house for now."

"Yes, please." He handed her the shopping bag. "It's heavier than I expected."

"That's because she bought me fancy boots to go with the dress. You can hang the garment bag in the coat closet. That'll keep the shirts from getting wrinkled."

"What about your dress? Shouldn't you hang that up before we leave?"

"Do I have time?"

"If you make it quick."

"I will." She headed down the hall. "My paperwork is on the table by the door if you want to double-check what I'm taking."

"Okay." After hanging up the garment bag, he walked to the small table by the door and flipped through the papers she'd stacked there. Her birth certificate was on top.

Katherine Adelaide Gifford. He'd never asked if *Kate* was a nickname. Or if she had a middle name. Her birth date wasn't a surprise, though. Millie had thrown a party for her in July.

He'd teased her about being eighteen months older than he was. They'd still been able to tease each other back then. The bachelor auction had changed that dynamic. Would it change back anytime soon? Would they be able to kid about this marriage?

Underneath the birth certificate was her divorce decree and under that a print-out of her social security info.

"That should do it, right?" She came out carrying a denim jacket and her shoulder purse. "I have my driver's license in my wallet."

"Then I think you're set." He handed her the papers.

"Good. Off we go."

He ushered her out the door and helped her into the front seat of his truck. She used to ride shotgun all the time, but she hadn't been in the passenger seat of his truck since the night he'd brought her home from the party after the bachelor auction. Two months of misery.

When he climbed behind the wheel, she glanced at him. "You washed it. And vacuumed the inside."

"Yes, ma'am."

"It looks very nice."

"Thank you." He turned the key and put the truck in gear. "Ever been to Choteau?"

"Never. Have you?"

"Oh, yeah. Charley and Henri brought all of us over there about a year after I signed on at the Buckskin. The town's on the Dinosaur Trail, and Charley was fascinated with those critters. He wanted us to see the museum. It has life-sized models."

"Sounds like the kind of educational trip I used to take in school."

"Sort of, only with a bunch of wranglers instead of school kids. Leo had just hired on that summer and you could tell he couldn't figure out why Charley would organize such an outing. He hadn't been here long enough to get it."

"Get what? I mean, dinosaurs are very cool, but—"

"Charley was a teacher at heart, and a natural father figure. He wanted to share something he loved with... well, people he cared about."

"I'm sad that I never got to meet him."

"I wish you could have, too. He would have loved you and vice versa."

"That museum sounds wonderful. Too bad we're crunched for time. I need to be home by five at the latest. Four-thirty would be better."

"Same with me. Guys are taking my shifts on Sunday. I don't want to show up late for barn duty this afternoon."

"You're working your regular shifts on Saturday?"

"I swapped out with Garrett so I'm on morning and he has afternoon. Henri moved some trail rides to Sunday and hired a couple of kids from Apple Grove High to handle feeding tomorrow night."

"She's like a field marshal in a military campaign. You should have seen her optimizing our shopping trip."

He grinned. "I'll bet. I would feel bad about throwing all this at her if I didn't know she relishes the challenge."

"Especially when she's pitted against a super-villain like Aunt Lilith."

"A super-villain? I know you don't like her, but—"

"Take my word for it. She'd give Lex Luther a run for his money."

"If you say so." He glanced at the papers she held in her lap. "Who nicknamed you Kate?"

"I did. When I was in kindergarten, I realized I had one of those names with a million variations. Either I picked one I liked, or I risked being saddled with one I hated. I told the teacher to call me Kate."

"I'll bet you did. I can see you marching up to her and announcing your decision. I wish I'd known you at five."

"When you were a toddler of three and a half?"

"I was always tall for my age. I could have passed for five."

She smiled. "I'm sure you could have. Is Rafe short for Rafael?"

"Yes, ma'am."

"Who shortened it?"

"The guys I hung out with and got into trouble with. They thought *Rafe* sounded badass. By the time I'd lost the urge to be badass, the name had stuck so I kept it."

"I can't imagine you as a troublemaker."

"I wasn't, but I was desperate for friends, a posse where I belonged. They could smell that desperation. I was big and strong, useful in a fight. They lured me in."

"Were you in fights?"

"Plenty. Then came the one where a guy was almost killed. The leader of our gang had a knife. If I hadn't stopped him, he would have slit that teenager's throat."

She shuddered. "So you left the group?"

"No, they kicked me out for interfering. Best thing that could have happened. I left town, turned into a saddle tramp and ended up here."

"How could I have known you for more than two years and never heard any of that?"

"It's not something you bring up when everyone's out to have a good time. Until I took you home from the party after the bachelor auction, we hadn't spent much time alone. We were always with the Buckskin gang."

"Huh. I guess you're right. Was that deliberate on your part?"

"Yes, ma'am. Sometimes I'd consider engineering more alone time. Then I'd remember the fire in your eyes and the steel in your voice when you announced you were never getting married again. I have no trouble picturing you laying down the law to your kindergarten teacher. No point in arguing with you when you speak with such conviction."

"Then why did you offer to take me home after the party two months ago?"

"You'd bid way more than you could afford so you could go on that ride with me. I thought the game had changed. I acted on that assumption."

"And that's my fault." She was quiet for a while after that. "You probably wonder why I bid so much."

"It's crossed my mind."

"You know the old expression, *dog in the manger*?"

"Yes, ma'am."

"That was me on the night of the bachelor auction. I was scared that I might win the all-day horseback ride with you and complicate the delicate balance we had going, but I couldn't bear the idea of some other woman winning you."

He took a deep breath. "I didn't want anyone else to win, either. Where does that put us, Kate?"

8

"I don't know." Kate glanced down at the papers in her lap. "Digging out my divorce decree reminded me of how complicated and traumatic it was trying to get out of that legal contract with Enrique."

Rafe sighed. "When I saw it listed as required paperwork, I figured seeing it again would be a downer."

"People who haven't been through it have no idea. You go into a marriage with all these hopes and dreams. Then if you discover you chose poorly, you're legally bound in ways you never thought about. And they act in ways you never expected."

"I talked to Leo this morning. He had an idea that might help ease your mind, but it would cost money."

"It's too late to get a prenup, if that's what he suggested. We don't have time."

"You can get the same thing afterward. It's called a post-nup. It would make our eventual..." He paused to cough. "Our divorce smooth as silk. I'll split the cost with you."

"You will?" She glanced at him in surprise. "Are you nervous about being legally tied to me?"

He kept his attention on the road as he gave a nonchalant shrug. "Sure I am."

"I don't believe you. You'd only be doing it to give me peace of mind. It's a good idea, though. I didn't realize such a thing was available."

"Me, either. I guess living in Southern California gave Leo an education about such things. Want to do it, then?"

"Yes, but since I'm the only one worried about this, I won't let you pay half. You're already taking on extra expense. And speaking of that, I'm paying for the license."

"No, you're not."

"Yes, I am."

"I looked it up. The groom is responsible for the license."

"Who cares? There's nothing traditional about this wedding, so why should you—"

"You're already saving me a whole bunch of money. If we were going the traditional route I'd be paying for a pricey rehearsal dinner at the Moose and an outrageously expensive trip to Lake Tahoe. Well, unless you'd set your heart on some other luxurious getaway."

Her heart was too busy aching to be set on anything. He'd thought about what a real wedding would have been like, even to the point of choosing where he'd take her on their honeymoon—a place she'd told him months ago was on her wish list.

"Hey, that was my lame attempt to lighten the mood. Clearly it was a misfire. Sorry."

"You remembered Lake Tahoe. I don't know exactly when I mentioned it, but not recently, that's for sure."

"I remembered it because I'd like to go, too. And I'm paying for the damned license. Letting you do it would hurt my manly pride. If that makes me unevolved, so be it."

She took a shaky breath. "Thank you, Rafe."

"It's not a lot of money. Besides, I'm still playing catchup after what you spent on the bachelor auction."

"It was for a good cause."

"So is this." He eased up on the gas as they neared the edge of town. "I have a vague idea where the courthouse is, but we don't have time to wander around. Would you pull out your phone and get me some directions?"

"Be glad to." She activated her phone's map feature and Rafe followed the voice cues, which took them straight to the courthouse.

He found a parking space, pulled in and switched off the engine. "Thanks."

"You're welcome."

"I'll get you out." He grabbed his paperwork from behind his seat and hurried around to the passenger side. Despite their tight timeline, she waited for him. She treasured his cowboy manners as much as he enjoyed demonstrating them.

He opened the door and held out his hand. "What are you smiling about?"

"You." She picked up her documents and put her hand in his. "You're more evolved than you think."

"How do you figure?"

"You asked for directions."

"That impressed you?"

"Sure did. A lot of guys would have gone with their vague idea and ended up lost."

"Then prepare to be impressed some more. It's a huge building and time's short." He squeezed her hand and released it. "Let's move out."

He wasn't kidding about moving out. She'd always been a fast walker, but she had trouble keeping up with his long strides. "Uh, Rafe, could you—"

"Sorry." He paused. "Guess I'm eager to get this over with."

"That makes two of us. Keep going. I just needed to catch my breath." As she fell into step beside him, she glanced up at the imposing façade. The handsome stone structure was the color of the baking powder biscuits she made nearly every morning for the guests. "Nice building."

"They meant for it to last, that's for sure."

"I like the style." She went through the door Rafe held for her. "And look at that staircase." Wide and graceful with polished wooden bannisters, it swept up to the main floor. If she had to take out a marriage license again, at least her surroundings had a touch of elegance.

"Up we go." True to his word, Rafe asked directions when they reached the reception desk and they easily found the office of the county clerk. A young couple was just finishing up as they arrived. Holding hands, the couple kept glancing at each other and smiling. Made her chest hurt.

When it was Kate and Rafe's turn, she learned that his middle name was Stephen, his mother's name was Lenora and his father was unknown. No wonder he'd soaked up the caring attention of Charley Fox.

The process was efficient and weirdly sterile considering what the license represented. Rafe paid the fee and handed the packet over to her before they walked out.

Desperate to change the focus, she glanced at her phone. "We almost have time to swing by the dinosaur museum."

"It's better if you go in. They have a dinosaur bone you can touch. We need to bring the license back to register it. Maybe we can go then."

"I'd like that." He was right to reject the idea. A drive-by wouldn't compare to the rich experience he'd had before. She'd just been looking for something to lift the somber mood that had settled over them.

She made sure she didn't drop the packet as Rafe handed her into the truck. Carefully extracting the license, she laid it on her lap, snapped a picture with her phone and emailed it to Aunt Lilith with a brief note—*wedding at four tomorrow, will send pictures and video.* Done.

Rafe swung into the driver's seat and closed the door.

"I just sent Aunt Lilith a picture of the license and told her the wedding was tomorrow. She might even mail a check to Ginny next week." Dragging in a breath, she let it out. "No backing out, now."

"I'd say the backing out time ended when we asked for the application form." He started the truck and eased out of the parking space. "How are you feeling?"

She took another deep breath. "Okay. You?"

"Okay." He flashed her a smile. "It's just a piece of paper, right?"

"Right." His smile looked forced. "Your middle name is Stephen, huh?"

"Yes, ma'am. My mom had two obsessions, Stephen King and first baseman Rafael Palmeiro. So I became Rafael Stephen."

"You said she *had* two obsessions, past tense. Does that mean she's no longer...."

"I honestly don't know. Maybe."

"Whoa." *Well done, Kate. Great topic.*

"Probably sounds harsh, but I had to disconnect for my own sanity. I spent less and less time at home as I got older. I'd moved out by the time I left town for good. Couldn't take the string of guys. It's not a pretty story."

"I'm sorry. I didn't mean to—"

"It's fine. The way I look at it, she gave me life. For a while there, I didn't know what to do with that gift, but now I do. I've found where I belong."

"I'd say so. The Buckskin gang would be lost without you." Just like that, he'd deftly steered them back to calmer waters. The guy had some life skills.

"No kidding. Who else can get stuff out of the cabinet over the fridge? Or clean the ceiling fans in Henri's place?"

Or agree to marry me? "That's what I'm talking about. You're indispensable."

"Damn straight." Discussing his adopted family clearly soothed him. "What about you, Katherine Adelaide? Are you named after anyone?"

"My mom just liked the name Katherine. She still calls me that instead of Kate. Adelaide was my grandmother's name. My dad's mom, or *mum* as she used to say. I loved listening to her accent."

"British?"

"Uh-huh. She was born in London and fell in love with my grandpa, who was an Air Force pilot. She came to this country after they were married. She willed me the teacups and teapot I use all the time."

"Does Millie know that?"

"She does. We talked about it when I unpacked them."

"That's what we get for spending so little time alone together. You don't find out as much about people when you're always in a group."

"Evidently not."

"Like for instance, I don't know if you like root beer floats."

"Who doesn't?"

"Leo can't stand 'em."

"How about you?"

"I could go for one right now. On the dinosaur museum trip, we picked up treats from a little place with a drive-through window. They made the best root beer floats I've ever tasted. But that was years ago. I didn't think to look for it on the way to Choteau. Too busy talking, I guess."

"A root beer float sounds great. I'll help you look. What was it called?"

"Teton Tasty Treats. It was painted robin's-egg blue with an orange roof."

"That should be easy to find."

"It's probably not there or I would have noticed it on the way over."

"Which side of the road?"

"This side. We stopped on the return trip."

"Is that when you found out Leo hates root beer floats?"

"Yep. Several of us ordered one but he got something else. I don't remember what, but I sure remember him carrying on about the evils of combining vanilla ice cream and root beer."

"That's funny. Does he still think that?"

"Probably. I can't remember the last time we fixed them at the bunkhouse. It's not something we ordinarily—"

"Rafe." She pointed to a speck of orange in the distance. "Could that be the place?"

"Might be. Keep your eye on it."

The orange spot grew bigger and turned out to be a peaked roof topping a small blue building. "I think that's it!" She so wanted it to be the same place. No wonder the root beer float had been the best one he'd ever tasted. He'd been on his first-ever family road trip.

"I see cars, so they're open." He sounded cautiously optimistic as he put on his turn signal.

"See? We could be in luck."

"The drive-through part looks the same." He pulled into line behind three trucks and an SUV. "Might be new owners, though."

"I'm going to believe it's the same owners and they still make terrific root beer floats."

He flashed her a smile. "Thanks for indulging me. We should still make it back by four-thirty."

"Even if it's five, that's okay. I'm glad you thought of this."

"I am, too. But in case they don't make those floats anymore, we should order something while we're here. What would you like as an alternative?"

"I'm not going to choose an alternative. They'll have floats."

He laughed. "Alrighty, then." The line moved and he pulled forward. "Can't see the order board yet." Rolling down the window, he leaned out and peered around the SUV. "Ha! Root beer floats are listed!"

"Told you."

"That you did." The SUV moved up. Easing the truck next to the two-way speaker, he put in their order. Then he glanced at her. "There's a shady spot around on the other side. Are you okay with parking there for a little while?"

"Absolutely. Is that what you did the last time?"

"That was Charley's idea. He wanted a chance to relax and enjoy our drinks. I think he was also worried about us spilling in his brand-new truck."

"You all fit in one?"

"No, we took Henri's, too. Everybody piled out of both trucks and gathered around a picnic table they had over there. Could be gone or somebody might be using it."

"It'll be there and vacant."

He grinned. "Okay." He pulled up to the window, paid for the drinks and handed the tall cups to her before driving slowly around the building. "I'll be damned. The picnic table is available."

"Told you."

"I don't remember this being a thing before."

"What?"

"You confidently stating the outcome you want. And being right, on top of it."

"I used to do that all the time before Enrique came along."

"Ah."

"I'm not sure why I did it just now. But it felt right."

"For the record, I like it."

"So do I."

Rafe parked in the shade of a stand of velvet green pine trees and aspens that had turned golden. Shutting off the engine, he came around to help her with the drinks.

When she stepped down, a cool breeze made her shiver. "I don't know about you, but I'm going to get my jacket."

"I'm fine. I'll hold your drink." He waited while she pulled her jacket out of the back seat and put it on. Retrieving her float, she walked with him over to a cement picnic table and benches anchored to a cement slab. The setup bore the mark of time, but somebody had cleaned the area recently.

He gestured toward the table. "Pick your spot."

"I want to sit so I can see the trees. The green and gold are spectacular." She settled down on the cool surface of the bench nearest to her.

"I want to sit so I can see you." He moved around to the other side. "Then I can tell if you really like this float or think it's just average."

"I'm going to really like it."

"I hope so, but there's a chance I oversold it."

"Nah, it'll be great." That cowboy sure could improve a view. He'd grabbed his hat when he'd climbed out of the truck and she'd dare anyone to find a man who looked better in a Stetson. His plaid Western shirt, a combination of brown, tan and burnt orange, highlighted the deep brown of his eyes.

He lifted his cup in her direction. "Here's to getting your sister to Johns Hopkins."

"I'll drink to that." She touched her cup to his before taking a sip. Creamy vanilla ice cream met the fizzy tang of root beer to create a party on her tongue. She swallowed. "Wow, this is *very* good. The ice cream must be homemade. Maybe the root beer, too."

"That's what Henri thought." He took a mouthful and his eyes lit up. After swallowing, he broke into a big grin. "Just like I remember. Maybe even better."

She savored the moment, ridiculously pleased that he'd been able to enjoy a root beer float like the one he'd shared with Charley, Henri and his brothers. "And here I thought this afternoon would be nothing but torture for you."

"Oh, it was back there in the courthouse. Filling out that document and knowing it meant virtually nothing was hell. But sitting here drinking root beer floats with you is heaven. It all balances out."

He had such a tender heart. "Are you sure?"

"Yes, ma'am. Don't worry about me, Kate. I've got this."

"Good to know." If only she believed him.

9

Chuck wagon stew, prepared by Jake and served on Friday night, had been a tradition at the bunkhouse for years. Now that most of the Brotherhood had moved out to live with their sweethearts, chuck wagon stew night had become even more important for keeping in touch.

Rafe had never sought the limelight when the Brotherhood gathered, but tonight he couldn't avoid it. Everybody wanted to talk about the wedding except Leo and Garrett, who knew all the details already and had made a quick trip into town for some reason or other.

Jake and CJ were busy in the kitchen making stew and baking hot rolls when Rafe and Nick came in from barn duty. Jake paused the cooking action so he and CJ could get the info on the trip to the courthouse.

Nick had already heard the story down at the barn, so he left to carry wood out to the fire pit. When Rafe got to the root beer float part of the story, CJ went bananas.

"Teton Tasty Treats is still in business?" He looked as if he'd won the lottery. "I'm taking Isabel up there as soon as we get an afternoon free."

"We're going where?" Isabel came in the back door with Millie. They'd been setting up places at the picnic table out by the fire pit.

"You have never had a root beer float like the one they make at this place." CJ turned to Jake. "Am I right?"

"They were good, but we were young and impressionable. Maybe they're not as epic as we remember."

"Yeah, they are," Rafe said. "Even better. Ask Kate when she gets here."

Millie glanced at him. "She's coming, right?"

"She is."

"Good. If this situation brings her back to the gang, that'll be a huge bonus."

"Yes, ma'am."

"We'll all work on it," Jake said. "And we'll schedule a group trip to Teton Tasty Treats soon, too. They might close for the winter so we'd better make it quick."

"That name sounds familiar," Millie said. "Is that the place you guys went right before I was hired? On the trip to the dinosaur museum?"

"That's it," Jake said. "We should do that, too. Recreate the entire trip, take everybody."

Rafe nudged back his hat. "It's a great idea, but the Buckskin operation's not the same as it was when we could leave Dusty in charge for a few hours. Now we have double the guest cabins and the raptor sanctuary to think about."

Jake was not to be deterred. "We'll figure it out, somehow. I'll talk to Henri."

"But enough about root beer floats and dinosaurs," Millie said. "I want to know how the rest of it went. Rafe, are you okay? Is Kate okay?"

"We got through it." Rafe gave a quick recap.

At the end of it, Millie nodded. "It sounds relatively painless. And you stopped off for root beer floats afterward. Good call."

"That took the sting out. Listen, I should go out and help Nick with the wood. I can't remember if we need to split some or not."

"Hang on, bro." Jake motioned to the front door as Matt and Lucy came in. "They'll want an update."

While Jake and CJ went back to cooking and Millie and Isabel went outside to check on Nick, Rafe told his story for the third time. It was beginning to sound canned, but that couldn't be helped. He'd just wrapped it up when Eva walked through the front door of the bunkhouse.

She headed straight for the kitchen. "Hey, guys, hey, Rafe." She tucked her peacock-blue hair behind her ears and smiled at him. "How'd it go today?"

"We got 'er done." It had become his stock phrase. "And this morning Henri picked up the rental clothes Nick and I need."

"Good. He was stressing about that. I told him Henri has it under control."

"Henri has *everything* under control," Lucy said. "I knew she was good at rallying the troops but I didn't understand the full scope of her powers until now."

Matt smiled. "She's impressive in full sail. You don't want to get in her way."

"That's for sure." Eva tucked her hands in the pockets of her jacket. "If there's anything she hasn't thought of, it's probably not important. She asked Josette and me if we'd be willing to come early tomorrow to do hair and nails for Henri, Millie and Kate. Naturally we agreed."

Rafe blinked. "Why do they need their hair and nails done?"

"It's a wedding."

"I guess I can see the hair styling for Millie. Hers is long enough that you can do that thing where you pile it up on her head. But Kate and Henri have short hair and I've never seen polish on Kate's nails."

"You will tomorrow. I didn't fancy up Kate's hair too much for Matt and Lucy's wedding, but this time she's the bride and I have some fun ideas, especially after Henri texted me a picture of Kate trying on her dress."

"You have a picture on your phone?" Lucy's eyes gleamed. "I'd love to see it."

"You and Matt can, but Rafe can't." She pulled it out of her small purse and walked over to show Lucy the picture.

"I won't look, either." Matt stepped away. "Brotherhood solidarity."

Rafe smiled. "Thanks."

Lucy took the phone and her eyes widened. "I *love* it. Gorgeous. She'll look amazing when she walks down the aisle in that."

Rafe had no doubt. She'd come toward him wearing her pretty new dress and her hair in some special arrangement. And it was all for show.

He'd promised her he would be fine and he would be, damn it. Even if it killed him. "Hey, I'll go see if Nick needs help with firewood."

"I'll go with you." Matt followed him out the back door and lowered his voice. "This sucks for you, bro."

"What else was I going to do? Let her marry some bozo who answered her ad in the *Gazette*?"

"You did what you had to, but I feel for you. Your wedding is supposed to be one of the best days of your life. Instead, at the end of the reception, she'll go one way and you'll go the other."

"At which point, I plan to start drinking."

"We'll all bunk down here tomorrow night. Keep you company."

"No, I can't let you do that. Leo and Garrett will be here. I don't need—"

"Yes, you do. Hey, weren't Millie and Isabel supposed to be out here? Nick's over by the fire, but I don't see the ladies." He raised his voice as they approached the fire pit. "Where'd you stash Millie and Isabel, Nick?"

"We're here." Millie's arm appeared over the back of one of the Adirondack chairs arranged in a semi-circle in front of the fire. She was holding a bottle of cider.

"Me, too." Isabel stuck up her arm from the chair next to it.

"Well, that's a relief." Matt walked over to the ice chest, pulled out two bottles and handed one to Rafe. "I get nervous when people disappear into thin air."

"We're just staking our claim to the Adirondacks. Isabel needs one because she's PG. And I'm saving this one for Kate." She pointed to her left.

"And the two on my right are reserved for Lucy and Eva," Isabel said.

"I see." Matt glanced at Nick. "Do you get one?"

"I'm next to Eva. That's my bottle on the ground by the chair leg." He grinned. "First come, first served, bro."

"Hey, Rafe." Millie looked up at him. "You should claim the one next to Kate. Go sit in it before Matt does."

"I don't want that one," Matt said. "I want the one next to Lucy."

"Sorry, dude." Isabel shook her head. "That's Eva's."

"I'll fix this," Nick took off his work gloves and stuck them in his back pocket, walked over to the chair he'd claimed and picked up his cider bottle. "Matt, you sit next to Lucy and I'll give Eva my chair. Then I'll take the one on her right."

"Perfect arrangement." Millie smiled.

Rafe stayed standing. "What about everybody else?" He glanced at Isabel. "What about CJ? Gonna make the father of your baby sit on a chummy stump?"

"Oh, he'd prefer that. These chairs would be terrible for playing his guitar. A chummy stump is way better."

Rafe shifted his gaze to Millie. "What about our hard-working chef in there? Your sweetheart Jake? And Leo and Garrett? They made the trip to Great Falls to buy the chairs."

"I'm not sure what to do about Leo and Garrett. You make a good point. But if Jake wants my chair, that's fine. I'll just sit on his lap."

"I like that idea." Nick exchanged a glance with Matt. "Are you thinking what I'm thinking?"

"That you're going to sit on my lap?"

Nick grinned. "We should do that. It would be worth it to see Eva and Lucy's faces."

"We're not doing that. We're going to act like normal people."

Millie giggled. "That'll take a lot of acting, Matt."

He rolled his eyes. "As I was saying. Nick, you invite Eva to sit on your lap and I'll invite Lucy to sit on mine. That frees up two chairs, so Leo and Garrett can each have one. Problem solved."

"I should get credit for solving it," Millie said. "The lap thing was my idea."

"I'll give you credit." Rafe took a seat, leaving one empty between him and Millie. Kate's chair. "And my thanks for taking on the extra work of this wedding tomorrow."

"No thanks needed. I'm happy to be there for you guys. We all are." She hesitated. "I guess you could ask Kate to sit on your lap, but I don't know it that's a good—"

"Probably not."

"We can say you each get a chair because you're wedding royalty."

"I guess, although I don't know if that works, either, now that you mention it. Maybe I should just take a chummy stump and let Jake have my chair."

"That's even more pointed, like you don't want to sit with her. You used to sit with her all the time."

"Millie's right," Nick said. "No worries if you each have a chair and the rest of us cozy up with our ladies. Sitting on your lap isn't something Kate would have done before, so no big deal if she doesn't do it, now."

"Hope so." Rafe heaved a sigh. "Tonight's going to be awkward, isn't it?"

"Maybe not. We've stashed in a good supply of cider. And awkward or not, we need to move beyond this rift that developed between Kate and us."

"We *will* move beyond it." Matt glanced over at Rafe. "I know the wedding isn't making it any easier, but I shudder to think what a mess this could be if Kate had ended up with somebody we barely know."

"Yeah," Nick said. "That would have been bad. For one thing, we wouldn't have wanted to be part of the wedding. If it had turned out she needed us to, I guess we would have done it, but this way, it's all in the family."

Rafe nodded. "That was my thinking." Except he hadn't been thinking at all when he'd raced over to her house last night. Faced with the specter of her marrying another man, he'd acted from a primitive instinct, throwing himself into the breach without considering the consequences.

And he'd do it again.

10

Kate cleaned the dining hall kitchen surfaces until she was in danger of scrubbing off the finish. Then she noticed a spot she'd missed and wiped down the entire counter again.

After sweeping the floor, she gave it a thorough mopping. Usually she let it air dry, but tonight she took off her boots, tossed down a couple of old towels and skated around on them until the floor was almost as shiny as the counters.

She was stalling. The trip to the courthouse had ended on a good note, but she'd been emotionally wiped out by the time Rafe had dropped her off at home. Her duties at the dining hall had been light, thank goodness—four couples who hadn't lingered. No complaints, there.

But she wasn't ready to face the Buckskin gang, much as she loved them and was grateful for their support. They were expecting her, though. Millie was counting on it, and this afternoon she'd confirmed with Rafe that she was going. Jake would have saved her some chuck wagon stew like he always used to.

Stripping off her gloves, she got her jacket from the storeroom and put it on before heading out the front door of the dining hall. Focused on her mission, she locked up quickly, pocketed her keys and started out, moving fast. Race walking would calm her jitters.

"Kate."

She swung around. "Rafe!" She pressed her hand to her wildly beating heart. "I didn't see—"

"Didn't mean to scare you." Hands shoved into the pockets of his open sheepskin coat, he stepped away from the corner of the dining hall. "I was waiting for you to finish up. Thought I'd walk you over, if that's okay."

"That's... very nice of you." She sucked in the cold night air as her breathing slowly returned to normal. He'd startled her, but that wasn't the only reason she was rattled.

Before the bachelor auction, she'd kept a low flame under her simmering attraction. Then he'd ridden into the arena at breakneck speed, a gorgeous man astride one of Ed's spectacular horses, and she'd reached the boiling point in seconds.

Two months later, she was still susceptible, particularly when he caught her off guard like this. His sheepskin coat made his shoulders look a mile wide and he had some end-of-the-day scruff going on. Hel-lo, sexy cowboy.

Had he buried his hands in his pockets so he wouldn't reach for her? Could be. That was why she'd kept her hands tucked away. Otherwise she was liable to grab him by the soft lapels of his coat and haul him in for a kiss.

She cleared the lust from her throat. "I hope you haven't been waiting long. I had some extra cleaning to do."

"Yeah, I figured you were stalling." He smiled.

"Why didn't you come in?"

"I wanted to let you take whatever time you needed."

"Did you think I'd wuss out? Because I wasn't going to."

"Figured that, too, which is why I'm here, to give you company on the way over. Thought it might help."

"It does. Thanks."

"I also wanted to give you a heads-up about a couple of things."

"Want to tell me on the way?"

"I'd rather tell you before we start out, in case... well, to begin with, we have eight new Adirondack chairs around the fire pit."

"Wow, when did that happen?"

"Yesterday afternoon. There was an end-of-season sale in Great Falls. Hard to believe it was only yesterday."

"I know what you mean. Yesterday seems like years ago. The chairs sound nice, though. You guys are such gentlemen I'm sure there's one saved for me, but I don't mind the chummy stumps."

"You'll have a chair and so will I, places of honor, in a way."

"Because of tomorrow?"

"Sort of. You know how you can have an un-birthday party?"

"Yeah."

"The gang's giving us an un-bachelor/un-bachelorette party. They want it to be festive, and we get our own chairs, but nobody's going to jump out of a cake naked."

She grinned. "Well, darn. That would have been something to see."

"Jake volunteered to do a cowboy striptease, but Millie—"

"What's that?"

"I've never seen one, but I think it involves getting down to a jock strap and chaps."

"Wow. The things I still need to learn about the wild West."

"You need breakaway pants, which Jake doesn't have."

"But clearly he wants some."

Rafe snorted. "Could be. Anyway, Millie nixed the idea for a lot of reasons, but mostly because this isn't a bachelor or bachelorette party. No strippers. No wedding talk. No jokes about weddings, wedding nights, or marriage in general."

"So what's different about tonight besides the chairs?"

"It'll just be... more festive. At least that's the idea. I had nothing to do with it. They cooked it up while we were gone this afternoon and didn't ask my permission on purpose, for fear I'd say no. Evidently they think we need a special party."

"Then we'd better make tracks." She started down the path at her usual brisk pace.

He fell into step beside her. "They'll be happy to see you."

"I'll be happy to see them. I was just dawdling because it'll be a little uncomfortable at first. There was the weirdness of our blowup and now the weirdness of this wedding."

"Everybody wants it to work."

She skidded to a stop. "*Our marriage?*"

"No, no! Our group, getting to where we can all hang out together again and everybody's relaxed."

"In other words, you and me back to our casual friendship mode."

"Right."

"I'd like that, too." She blew out a breath and continued down the path. "Sorry I came unglued. If I ever thought there was a secret plan to turn this wedding into an actual marriage, I'd—"

"No such plan. Believe me, I asked. I can tell when they're up to something and they're not. Everyone respects your stand on marriage, including me."

"You do?"

"Yes, ma'am."

"You don't think I'm—how did you put it two months ago? A damn coward who's willing to let one lousy experience rule her life forever?"

He winced. "I had no business saying that and I apologize."

"Thank you."

"I haven't been in your shoes. I didn't go into a marriage with stars in my eyes and come out with two black eyes."

"That's a colorful way of putting it."

"I should have clarified why you bid on me at the bachelor auction. I didn't realize...."

"What?"

"You were just hot for my body." There was a hint of a smile in his voice.

Could they tease each other about this? Maybe. "I wasn't the only woman thinking that. You've got it goin' on, cowboy. That bidding was fierce."

"Surprised the hell out of me."

"Did you take note of who else was bidding?"

"No."

"Well, I did. I could draw you up a list of who—"

"No, thanks. I'll soon be a married man."

"Cut out the *married man* nonsense. You're free to date. That's part of the deal."

"Will you?"

"Um... sure...."

"That didn't sound very convincing. Tell you what. You first. Start going out with someone and I'll follow your example."

"You shouldn't wait for me. I'm not all that fond of the dating game."

"That makes two of us."

"But how else are you going to find someone who wants the same things you do?"

"Maybe she'll just show up. Lucy came back to the Buckskin after years away and reunited with Matt."

"Is there an old flame of yours who might drop in unexpectedly?"

"Not that I remember."

"And you would remember. You have a memory like an elephant."

"Isabel arrived out of the blue and CJ—"

"Not out of the blue. For a wedding. Is that your strategy? Wait for the next wedding and hope you fall for someone in the bridal party?"

"It could happen."

"Waiting for someone to magically appear is not realistic."

"Worked for Matt and CJ."

"You need to be proactive. Your temporary marriage to me would give you time to learn whether the person you're dating is the right one, since you can't rush into that legal trap like some do. Like I did. You could use the time to your advantage and start exploring."

"Or I could wait for someone to show up."

She groaned. "Meanwhile your sperm is losing motility."

"What?"

"You haven't heard that?"

"No, and I can't believe we're discussing my sperm."

"It's a fact, Rafe. Sperm motility declines after twenty-five. You turned thirty this year. You're on the downhill slope, my friend. And if you want kids, you—"

"My sperm is up to the job, thank you very much."

"Maybe, but the clock is ticking. Besides, even if you started dating someone this weekend, it would take weeks before you had sex and weeks more before you'd evaluated whether she'd make a good partner."

"I won't start dating someone this weekend. I have a wedding to attend."

"I'm aware of that." The lantern by the front door of the bunkhouse shone through the trees and the sound of CJ's guitar drifted from the picnic area in the back.

"As for the rest of your timetable, who gave you a crystal ball?"

"It's a calculated guess I made from observing that you're cautious and methodical." She liked that about him.

"No, I'm not. When I heard your gonzo plan of putting an ad in the *Gazette*, I was at your doorstep within minutes offering myself as an alternative. There's nothing cautious or methodical about that."

"Everybody acts out of character sometimes." She stepped into the pool of light by the front door and turned to him. "But the fact remains that in general, you—"

"Hang on." He faced her and shoved back his hat. "If you have no interest in marriage and kids, why are you such a sperm motility expert?"

Trust him to zero in on that. "I *used* to want a family."

"Aha." He pointed a finger at her. "Then that's *another* thing you've—"

"Yep. No kids for me. I'm past thirty, like you, and age is even more critical for women."

"But you can still have them, right?"

"I can, but I won't." She looked him square in the eye. "My research isn't doing me any good, but if it lights a fire under you, my efforts won't be wasted."

"I didn't know you wanted a family." His gaze searched hers. "It seems wrong that you've given up when you could still—"

"You're entitled to your opinion. I'm not changing my mind."

His jaw tightened. "We could get in a fight over this point."

"Probably."

"Let's not."

"Yeah, let's not." She took a breath. "Do you need to go in the house for any reason?"

"No."

"Then let's do this thing." She took the alternate route to the fire pit, walking around the end of the bunkhouse. Then she stopped. "Oh, Rafe, that's so pretty! What's making those sparkly lights in the trees out by the fire pit?"

"Leo stopped by the hardware store and got one of those projectors that gives you the sparkly effect. Had to buy a couple of long-ass cords to connect to an outlet at the house, but the result is worth it."

"He did that just for this party?"

"Well, he wanted it for tonight, but we can use it other times."

"What a sweetheart he is."

"You have a lot of fans in this group, Kate."

Her throat tightened. "I'm getting that. It's humbling."

"Ready to join the party?"

"So ready." She hurried up the path. "Hey, you guys! We're here!"

CJ stopped playing, and the group erupted from the semi-circle of chairs, laughing and calling her name. As the Buckskin gang surrounded her in an epic group hug, she vowed to keep this connection strong. No matter what.

11

While everyone fussed over Kate, Rafe took off his coat and laid it with the others piled on the picnic table. The blazing logs in the fire pit kept the area warm enough that nobody needed them.

The group's enthusiastic response to Kate pricked his conscience. She needed this connection and she'd denied herself because of him. No sugarcoating that truth.

When Jake left to heat up Kate's serving of chuck wagon stew, Rafe went with him. He'd claimed they needed a couple more bags of chips and Jake couldn't carry everything. Not a plausible excuse, but nobody questioned it.

As they walked back to the house, he lowered his voice, although the group's rowdiness would likely drown out whatever he said. "I feel like a first-class a-hole, bro."

"Why? You're the hero, the guy who's agreed to—"

"It's the least I can do after the way I've acted the past two months. She tried to hang out with the gang after our big fight, remember?"

"She did, but I figured it became too awkward for her." Jake took the steps quickly and went through the back door to the kitchen.

Rafe followed him in. "Which is my fault. "Whenever she showed up, I sulked."

"You were upset. And rightly so." Jake dished stew into a small pan, set it on a burner and turned on the heat.

"Yeah, and I wanted her to know it." Rafe scrubbed a hand over his face. "I'll bet she stopped coming because of my standing in the group. If I was unhappy because of her, she was the one who should bow out."

"Maybe. If that's what she figured, she read the situation right. Our first loyalty is to you." Grabbing a wooden spoon, Jake stirred the contents of the pan. "And she'd bid aggressively to get you. We all thought that was a promising sign."

"I could have started an affair with her that day."

Jake kept stirring.

"You knew that, didn't you?"

"She told Millie. Millie told me." He glanced at him. "Wish you had?"

"Sometimes. Except it would have been on her terms. No sleeping over, no leaving my stuff at the cottage. She wanted me in her bed but not in her life."

"That ex must have been a piece of work."

Rafe grimaced. "I wouldn't mind going a few rounds with Enrique Caputo."

"That's his name?"

"Yeah. Saw it on the divorce decree today."

"You'd really like to punch him out?"

"Yes."

"That's big, coming from someone who wouldn't hurt a fly."

"I hate him."

"I get that. But if he'd been a model husband, we'd never have met Kate."

"Which would've been sad for us, although we wouldn't know what we were missing. But she'd have the life she'd expected and the kids she wanted."

"She wanted kids?"

"Just found that out a few minutes ago."

"Huh. I thought she and her famous chef husband were focused on making names for themselves in the restaurant world." Jake got down a bowl and a plate. "Would you grab me a box of crackers?"

"Sure." He got one out and handed it over. "She probably wanted that, too, but being famous doesn't rule out having kids. She wanted them bad enough that she researched sperm motility."

"Sperm whatzit?" Jake put the bowl on the plate and piled some crackers around it.

"It's a measure of how fast those little dudes swim to the finish line."

"You can measure that?"

"Evidently."

"How?"

"I didn't ask. It's the sort of discussion that could strike a match, if you know what I mean."

Jake laughed as he scooped the stew into the bowl. "Oh, do I ever! When I want to get Millie hot, I bring up sperm motility. Works every time."

"Okay, not the term itself, but the concept of how sperm moves into—oh, hell, never mind."

Grinning, Jake picked up the plate and handed it to him. "See if you can deliver this steaming bowl of stew to your lady without striking any matches. I'll snag the potato chips."

"Oh, right. Forgot about those."

"Understandable." Jake pulled two bags of chips from the cupboard. "When a guy's fixated on sperm motility, he can't be expected to—"

"Make jokes if you want, but your motility peaked at twenty-five."

"You don't know that."

"Statistics, bro." He turned and headed for the back door. "That's the average age it happens. Since all of us have either turned thirty or are fast approaching it, we—"

"Tell that to CJ. His motility may have peaked five years ago, but his aging sperm got past that condom, no problem."

"Maybe he's the exception or just got lucky." He went out the back door and left it open for Jake.

"Oh, he got lucky, all right. Isabel adores him. He's at the top of his game. Even plays that guitar better than ever." Jake shut the door behind him.

"I agree with you there." CJ had launched into *Chattahoochee*, one of his favorites. "Anyway, this motility issue is a wake-up call if you want kids. I figure you and Millie do."

"Eventually."

"But if you wait too long, it might be more difficult for Millie to get pregnant."

"Meaning we'd have to have sex more often to accomplish the task?"

"I suppose that's logical, but—"

"Then I don't see a problem." Jake chuckled. "My sperm can take its own sweet time."

"I hadn't thought of that." He could use Jake's argument with Kate, except another discussion along that line would be unwise.

"Like Charley used to say, there's always two sides to a situation. Unless there's more than two."

"I was missing him today at the Teton Tasty Treats."

"Bet you were. We'll schedule that trip. Just have to get this wedding over with and we'll have time to plan it."

"Sounds good." Except once the wedding was over he wouldn't have all these great excuses to spend time with Kate.

She glanced up with a smile as he approached with her dinner. "That looks and smells delicious."

"Sorry you've been missing out for weeks."

"No worries. I'm here, now." She took the plate and balanced it on her lap.

"How're you doing on cider?"

"Still have half a bottle."

"Then I'll get myself one and be back." He walked over to the ice chest and pulled out a chilled bottle as CJ finished playing *Chattahoochee* and paused for a gulp of cider.

"Great job, bro," Rafe said.

"Thanks." CJ smiled. "It's fun. This next one should get everybody on their feet." He launched into Kip Moore's *Somethin' 'Bout a Truck*, the gang's new singalong favorite.

"The truck song!" Isabel pushed herself from her chair, belly and all, and started dancing solo. Eva wiggled out of Nick's lap, singing the bouncy lyrics as she pulled him to his feet. Matt and Lucy joined them, followed quickly by Millie and Jake. Leo and Garrett took turns dancing with Isabel.

Kate remained seated, her dinner in her lap. Kate in wallflower mode startled and saddened him. She used to be the life of the party.

Made sense that she was still in her chair. The truck song was a recent tradition and she likely hadn't learned the words.

Leo and Garrett felt comfortable dancing with Isabel, whose partner was providing the music, but they'd hesitate to invite Kate to dance after he'd made a point of fetching her from the dining hall. Getting her on her feet was his job.

Threading his way through the dancers, he set his bottle on the ground by his chair. "Come on." He took away her stew, leaving the plate on the arm of her chair. Pulling her up, he started singing and moving with the music.

With a bemused smile, she danced with him, tentative at first, as if they'd never done this before. But the lyrics were easy and addictive. She began singing along, getting into it.

Gripping her firmly around the waist, he twirled her around in a dramatic show of strength like he used to when they'd danced as friends. She laughed.

Much better. Gradually she shed her hesitation and became the Kate he used to know. Giving herself up to the rhythm, she added a few wiggles and shimmies that made his mouth go dry.

When the song ended, she was breathing hard. "Thanks. Guess I'll need to learn all the words if the truck song is a thing, now."

"It's a thing." His heart was thumping like an engine that had thrown a rod.

"What else has changed since I was here last?"

I'm more in love with you than ever.

12

Rafe had saved her from being odd woman out. Kate was grateful, but the episode showed her that weaving herself back into the fabric of the Buckskin gang would be tricky. What was that old saying? *You can never step in the same river twice.*

Chuck wagon stew night was the same and not the same. Adirondack chairs had replaced most of the chummy stumps. CJ had learned a new song and everyone had picked up the lyrics. Isabel's belly had grown bigger.

When CJ had started playing the truck song, Eva had pulled Nick out of his chair so he'd dance with her. Two months ago, she wouldn't have been here. Now she was an accepted part of the gang, more secure in her role than Kate was.

The bachelor auction had changed everything, including this group she loved. She and Rafe were still considered a couple, but their dynamic had become way more complicated since August. Nobody knew how to treat the new entity that was Rafe and Kate. How could they? She didn't know, either.

"Hey, everybody!" Millie clapped her hands like a teacher on the playground. "The truck song just gave me an idea. Who's up for musical chairs with live music?"

Jake gazed at her. "We've never done musical chairs."

"Wouldn't it be fun, though?"

"Depends on what you mean by fun." Matt smiled. "There's a reason we've never played. The guys will be eliminated first because a cowboy is hard-wired to give up his chair to a woman."

"You'd have to set aside your training just this once," Millie said. "I'd be fascinated to see if you can do it."

"I'd love to play," Kate said, "once I finish my stew."

"Oh, right." Millie glanced her way. "I forgot you still have food. Isabel, I didn't think about you, either. This might be the wrong game for—"

"Are you kidding? It's the perfect game for me. I'm a pregnant lady, so I'll be treated like I'm made of glass. I do think Matt has a point. They won't fight us for the chairs."

"But if you want to try it," Matt said, "I'm willing. We'll all lose, but that's okay."

"Maybe one of us could win." Jake had a gleam in his eye. "This game is more about strategy and finesse. If we can get over our instinct to give up our chair, we might have a chance."

"That's a big *if*," Matt said.

Nick looked confused. "We have to take chairs away from women? That doesn't sound like a very good game."

"You've never played?" Eva gave him a surprised glance.

"No, ma'am."

"It's a classic. We should do it at least once, just so you can see what it's like."

"It'll be an adventure in social dynamics," Millie said. "Is everyone willing?"

"Sure." Jake gave his wife a quick kiss. "Set us up."

"Okay, then. Kate, we'll arrange the rest of the chairs while you finish your dinner. We'll put yours in last."

"Ladies, stand down, please." Jake cast a glance around the semi-circle. "The men will arrange the chairs. Let us demonstrate our cowboy manners before we turn around and blow them to smithereens."

"We won't blow them to smithereens." Matt grabbed two chairs. "But it'll be fun to see which of the ladies wins."

"We need to fill in with chummy stumps." Lucy picked up one.

"Two will do it." Eva took the stump Nick had been using as a footstool.

CJ strummed a few chords on his guitar. "What tune do you want?"

Everyone shouted *the truck song* except Kate. But at least she was in the know.

And she'd made it here for the first, and possibly the one and only, game of musical chairs. Chances were good it would become a memory everyone referred to later.

By the time she finished her stew and most of the crackers, the circle was complete except for her chair. She picked up her plate and empty cider bottle and stood. "You can have mine, now."

Rafe came to fetch it and Jake took her plate, bowl and empty cider bottle. She joined the group that was gathered around Nick.

He listened intently as Millie explained the rules.

"And no shoving."

He stared at her in horror. "I would *never* shove a woman."

"What about jostling?" Lucy grinned at Matt. "We can all jostle each other, right?"

His eyebrows lifted. "There's a fine line between shoving and jostling."

"There's a very substantial line, Matt," Millie said. "You shove with both hands and put your whole body into it. That's not allowed, since you guys have more upper body strength than we do. You jostle with your hip and try to scoot someone sideways."

Jake laughed. "I'm all for hip action. Jostle away, Millie."

"So body contact is okay?" Nick still looked reluctant.

"A friendly nudge is allowed," Eva said.

"But that doesn't seem fair." Nick frowned. "I can nudge with more force than you can."

"But you won't use that extra strength against a woman," Matt said, "which is what I'm saying. The ladies are sure to win because we can't go all out."

Millie, Lucy and Eva insisted that wasn't necessarily true, while Nick and Rafe backed up Matt's statement.

Garrett raised his voice above the hubbub. "We can do a second round with just the guys, no holds barred."

"That's a good idea," Millie said. "We can have one with just the women, too."

"No need for that," Matt said. "That's what this first round will turn into."

CJ tapped a quick *ba-DUM-dum* on his guitar. "I want in on the guys-only version."

Leo turned around. "But we need music, bro."

"We could use the extra-long extension cord to plug in those speakers you bought for your phone."

"Good thinking."

"But you'll play for the coed round, I hope," Millie said. "That'll make it way cooler."

"Oh, I'm definitely doing that. Let me know when you're ready."

"First, I want to mix up the couples." Millie took charge, as she often did.

She was the lynchpin of the group. The past few weeks without chuck wagon stew night, bunkhouse poker games and outings to the Moose, Millie had been Kate's lifeline with phone calls and chats over afternoon tea. Tomorrow she'd be the maid of honor at Kate's peculiar wedding. Couldn't have a better friend than that.

"Kate, you get between Leo and Garrett."

"Aye-aye, cap'n." She took her place in line behind Leo.

He turned to smile at her. "Good to have you back."

"Thanks."

"You up for poker next week?"

"Sure. Just let me know."

"Nick's available when Eva has girls' night with her friends. Probably Wednesday, but I'll find out for sure and let you know. That'll give us five players for a change."

"Count me in." Rafe would be there, of course. By slightly turning her head, she had a view of him across the circle of chairs.

He laughed at something Eva said. Then she made another comment and he totally lost it. She used to make him laugh like that. Damn, she missed those days.

"Ready, CJ!" Millie called out.

He started playing and Kate followed Leo around the circle—eleven people for eight chairs and two chummy stumps. The music stopped and Kate plopped right into the chair next to her. Leo got a chummy stump. Isabel grabbed a chair behind Kate, leaving Garrett standing, his smile resigned.

He lifted both hands. "Matt's right. Couldn't do it, especially to a pregnant lady. I'll go keep CJ company."

Millie removed the chummy stump Leo had used and adjusted the circle before calling out to CJ again. When the music stopped, Kate dodged right and stole the chair from Leo, but he slid neatly into the one Jake was going for.

Jake sat on his lap and grinned at Kate. "This counts, right?"

"Afraid not, Skippy."

"Then it's the losers' circle for me." He walked over to stand next to Garrett.

Rafe was the next one out, followed by Matt. Nick was eliminated, and finally, Leo.

Matt swept a hand toward the row of guys. "Did I call it or what?"

"Admit it, though," Millie said. "You had fun."

"Big fun," Jake said. "It's not every day I get to sit in Leo's lap."

"Looks like it's down to us girls." Lucy said. "May the best woman win."

"Tough competition." Millie grinned. "But I can take you guys."

"Hang on," Kate said. "I need to stretch."

That got her a laugh as she did a couple of quick lunge poses. Two months ago, she would have given her all to this game. She'd always been competitive and proud of it.

But Millie was her best friend. Lucy had given her a raptor sketch for donating so much money to Raptors Rise. Isabel was taking time from her just-opened coffee shop to attend the wedding. Eva was styling her hair painting her nails for free tomorrow.

CJ launched into the train song, and the five of them circled four chairs. When he stopped playing, she made a show of battling Millie for a chair, but even Millie knew she wasn't trying very hard. Millie claimed the chair, but then she got up and hugged Kate. "Go get some cider. I'll be there soon."

Garrett removed another chair and Kate headed over to the group of guys. "There's method to my madness. One woman, seven cowboys. I'll take those odds any day."

Rafe smiled. "Want cider?"

She batted her eyes at him. "Yes, please, kind sir."

"Have a seat." Garrett positioned the chair he brought over so she had a view of the competition.

"Thank you, Garrett. Much obliged."

Jake produced an open bag of chips. "Welcome to the losers' circle. It's better here."

"I can see that. While they're running around in a circle, you're drinking cider and eating chips."

"Hit it, CJ!" Millie called out and the four women circled three chairs.

CJ abruptly stopped playing when Isabel was perfectly positioned to drop into a chair and Lucy lost out.

Matt stared at him. "Did you just cheat?"

CJ's expression was serene. "I didn't *just* cheat. I've been helping Izzy from the beginning. If you can't give a boost to the love of your life, the mother of your child, the sunshine in your days, the—"

"Okay, okay, I get it."

"You'd do the same."

"I would if I could play a guitar." When Lucy came over, Matt wrapped an arm around her shoulders. "I need to inform you that CJ's making sure Isabel's in front of a chair before he stops playing."

She laughed. "Of course he is. We figured that out after the second round. Isabel will win. The real battle is for second place."

"Eva's gonna take it," Nick said.

"Oh, yeah?" Jake puffed out his chest. "Then you don't know Millie."

Garrett removed another chair and Millie gave the signal to CJ. Nick and Jake shouted encouragement as Eva, Millie and Isabel circled the back-to-back chairs. Millie grabbed one of them a split-second before Eva did. Jake executed an elaborate victory strut while Nick swung Eva into his arms and showered her with praise for lasting this long.

Millie rose from her chair and faced the group. "I concede to Isabel, since we all know she'll win with CJ playing guitar. And why shouldn't she? In about twelve weeks she'll give birth to the first Buckskin baby born in Apple Grove. Let's hear it for our musical chairs champion, baby-momma Isabel!"

Kate cheered along with everyone else. She was excited about this baby. Maybe not as excited as Henri, who'd proclaimed herself a grandma from CJ's side of the family. The men of the Brotherhood would be honorary uncles to little Cleo Marie.

Millie and Lucy would be aunties, along with Eva, now that she and Nick were a committed couple. Kate's connection was more tenuous than theirs, but this was her adopted family and she'd claim an auntie role, too. She shouldn't have given up her connection with the group so easily two months ago.

Now that she was back in the fold, all she had to do was keep her relationship with Rafe on an even keel. She could do that, right?

13

Playing musical chairs with seven toasted cowboys was a recipe for disaster. But CJ wanted to do it, so Rafe grabbed two chairs and added them to the two still out there.

Nick brought two more. "This would be a lot easier with folding chairs." He helped Rafe create a reasonable facsimile of a circle.

"I like using these chairs." Leo surveyed the arrangement. "Once you're in them, you have a lock on that space. With folding chairs, you can shove somebody off the seat."

"No shoving," Nick said. "Millie said."

CJ took a gulp from his cider bottle. "That rule was for the ladies."

"Oh, yeah?" Garrett nudged back his hat. "Will you be shoving, then?"

CJ smiled. "I might." He drained his bottle. "Okay, let's do this. I picked the tune and Millie's set to operate the music."

Matt joined them. "I just asked Millie what the song was. Good choice, bro."

"What'd you pick?" Rafe wouldn't mind a change. He liked the train song, but he liked a lot of other ones, too.

"*American Girl*, Carrie Underwood. Makes me think of Cleo Marie and Izzy."

Rafe smiled. "Nice." Maybe this game wouldn't be a total snafu, after all.

"Let me get rid of this bottle and we can start."

"I'm pumped." Jake spit into the palms of both hands and rubbed them together.

Leo snorted. "What the hell was that for?"

"You'll see. I have a strategy."

"Just don't be grabbing me with hands you spit on. That's gross."

"I vote no grabbing at all," Nick said. "I think we should outlaw shoving, too."

Jake shrugged. "Fine with me. Won't affect my game plan."

CJ came back and after some discussion about the lineup order and whether shoving was allowed, Rafe ended up behind Jake and in front of Nick.

"Hey, guys," Nick called out. "Are we going the same speed as we did with the women?"

"Nah." Jake shook his head. "We need to ramp it up. Let's run around these chairs."

"The circle's too tight," Rafe said, "and so are you."

"Spoilsport. I'm gonna jog, then. Try to keep up."

"Okay, Millie," Matt called out. "Hit it!"

Jake started off at a fast trot. Without breaking stride, he picked up a chair, held it over his head and shouted *I can't lose!*

When Millie stopped the music, Jake flipped over his chair and plopped into it, grinning.

A chorus of protests erupted as the rest of them gathered around Jake and tried to drag him out of the chair.

He gripped the chair arms, planted his feet and continued to smile. "Nobody said I couldn't. This is my chair and I'm keeping it."

Rafe glanced at Nick. "Feel like doing a little lifting?"

"As a matter of fact."

In one swift motion, Rafe took one side and Nick the other one. Before Jake could react, they picked up the chair and carried him, yelling his head off, to the sidelines.

"Keep him there, Millie," Rafe said.

"Will do." Millie settled into Jake's lap. "Kate, you'll have to run the music. I have my orders."

Jake laughed. "How do you intend to keep me here, sweet lady?"

"With my feminine wiles." And she kissed him.

Kate whooped. "Well done, Millie!" She glanced at Rafe. "Nicely handled. I'll start the music whenever you guys are ready."

Five chairs and six guys. Garrett was eliminated next, then Leo. Rafe figured out that Kate stopped the music whenever the word *heart* was in the lyrics. Conscious or unconscious, it was a tell.

By concentrating on that word, which popped up in the refrain, he beat out CJ for a chair. Then Matt. He and Nick circled the last chair.

The word *heart* was coming. He would be in position and Nick would lose. He quickened his step, got past the front of the chair and was headed behind it when Kate stopped the music.

Nick dived for the chair and threw up his hands in triumph. "I won!" He jumped out of the chair and turned to Rafe. "I can't believe it!"

Rafe shook his hand and grinned. "Good job, Nicholas."

Eva hurried over, all smiles as she presented him with a cold bottle of cider, acting like it was a trophy. "For the musical chairs champion. And on only the second time you played, too."

Rafe carried the empty chair back to the group while Nick basked in his winner's status. Everybody pitched in to rearrange the semi-circle and CJ picked up his guitar to play another song.

Taking the seat she'd been assigned originally, Kate sipped from a bottle of cider. Rafe grabbed what was his last one of the night and settled in beside her.

She glanced over at him, her voice pitched low. "I thought for sure you had it."

"Lost focus." He shrugged. "It happens."

"Until that last round, it seemed like you knew in advance when I'd stop the music. Was that my imagination?"

He shook his head.

"Were you reading my mind?"

"You always stopped on the word *heart.*"

"I did?"

"I know that refrain. I could anticipate when the word was coming up and make sure I was in position."

"I'll be damned. Did you really lose focus at the end?"

He met her gaze and smiled.

"You wanted him to win."

"Yeah. It's a small thing, but—"

"Small kindnesses are what make the world go 'round."

The soft light in her gray eyes made his breath hitch. "You're so beautiful, Kate." Whoops. Hadn't meant to say that. He looked away. "Sorry. Lost my head."

"No need to apologize." Her low voice had a sexy vibe.

She probably hadn't intended to sound that way. "But it would be better if I don't go around saying things like that."

"I suppose."

He cleared his throat. "Did you get any response from your aunt about the picture of the marriage license?"

"Yes. She texted back *Good start. Eager for pictures of tomorrow's wedding.*"

"I know we're not supposed to discuss this subject tonight, but I feel a little out of the loop. Is everything set?"

"Except for one thing. I realized while I was making dinner for the guests that we don't have rings."

"Yikes. I don't wear any so I completely spaced that. Any ideas?"

"Not at this late date. I don't wear them, either. They get in the way for someone who cooks all the time. But Aunt Lilith will expect one of those typical pictures of two hands, each wearing an appropriate wedding ring."

"We could take a picture of Lucy's and Matt's hands. Who would know?"

"That's a good idea, except the exchanging of rings is part of the ceremony which will be on the video."

"Which will be done by Red, who makes jewelry."

"That's true." Kate glanced at him. "Does she make rings, though?"

"I'm not sure, but I'll bet she has some. If a person's into jewelry, they'd be into all of it, wouldn't they?"

"Makes sense."

"Let me check with Red in the morning. I'll have more time than you will. I don't have to get my hair done."

"Are you sure? Eva might want to give you a quick trim, maybe add some gel to give you a spiky look for the ceremony."

He stared at her. "A spiky look? Since when have I—"

"You should see your face." Her eyes twinkled. "You'd think I'd suggested you show up naked."

"Gelled, spiky hair is just one step removed from showing up naked, in my case. Which reminds me, I was thinking of wearing my hat. My good one. Nick has one that's almost exactly like it, so we could have a unified look."

"You can if you want. But a hat would make the *now you may kiss the bride* part more difficult."

"Am I going to kiss you?"

Pink tinged her cheeks. "I think you have to. For the video."

"Oh, well. A guy's gotta do what a guy's gotta do."

"Will you mind it so much?"

"What do you think?"

"I honestly don't know. Our one and only kiss changed everything between us. You might not want to go there ever again."

"Or I might cherish the moment. I might be looking forward to one last chance to kiss you, even if it's only for the video."

Her breath caught.

He didn't miss that little intake of breath. "Let's turn this around. How do you feel about having to kiss me… for the video?"

"I don't know." The glow of excitement in her eyes was unmistakable.

"Oh, I think you do. You just don't want to tell me." He was on the verge of asking to drive her home. He wanted more time alone with her before tomorrow. He saw something in the depths of those gray eyes, something that gave him hope that they—

"Kate?"

He glanced up as Millie and Jake came toward them. What lousy timing.

"We're heading home," Millie said. "You must be exhausted. How about if we give you a ride?"

She stood immediately. "That's a great idea. Thank you. I'll get my jacket."

He stood, too. "I'll get it."

"No worries. I'll grab it on my way out." She flashed him a quick smile. "Let me know what Red says. See you tomorrow."

And just like that, she was gone. Leaving with Millie and Jake made sense. Her cottage was only slightly out of their way. But she'd agreed damned fast, as if she'd wanted to escape.

Maybe the simmering heat in his body wasn't going on in hers. But her eyes said differently. And her rapid departure could mean that she didn't trust herself to stick around.

Two months ago, she'd wanted to have an affair. Was he a fool not to revisit that idea and see what happened?

So what if she'd said he couldn't stay the night? She had no idea how she'd feel after they'd made love. It might cause her to do a complete one-eighty.

Or not. She was stubborn. But so was he.

14

Her wedding day. Kate was awake and roaming the house turning on lights long before the sun was up. The ceremony wasn't until four, a long nine hours away.

She had nothing to do until ten this morning, when the Babes, Millie and Isabel would gather at Henri's. Henri had given her the day off as a kindness. But work was her therapy and she could use some right now.

Cooking a big breakfast would occupy the time, except she wasn't hungry. Coffee would be good, though. She made a pot and got out the brownies.

Fetching a blanket and putting on her slippers, she set herself up on the porch with a mug of coffee and a plate of brownies. She never had brownies for breakfast. She'd never come out to the porch in her nightgown to watch the sunrise, either.

Considering what this day had in store, she might as well start it this way. Wrapped in her favorite blanket, a light blue one that was incredibly soft, she snuggled into the roomy contours of the Adirondack chair and sipped her coffee.

This chair creaked a lot more than the new ones Leo and Garrett had brought back from Great Falls. Millie had told her this one and its mate had been on the porch when she'd moved in ten years ago. She'd repainted them at some point and they needed it again—in Millie's opinion. Kate didn't mind the shabby chic look of faded green paint.

By the time she'd finished a brownie, the sky had lightened to a dove gray and the porch light winked out. A few little birds chittered in the tree near the porch. Up the hill, all was dark in Henri's two-story.

Gravel crunched. Footsteps. She made a guess before a figure emerged from the shadow of the trees near the parking area. "Hey, Rafe."

"Hey, Kate." He moved closer and peered at her. "Why are you out here?"

"Felt like it."

"How come?" He came to the bottom of the steps, his hands in the pockets of his sheepskin coat.

"Needed some air."

He nodded as if that made sense. "I smelled coffee so I figured you were up. Thought you'd be inside, though."

"Want a cup?"

"Yes, ma'am, if you don't mind." He climbed the steps.

"Help yourself. I'm all tucked in, here."

"I see that." He looked amused. "Need a refill?"

"Sure."

Crossing the porch, he went inside. Soon he was back, a mug of coffee in one hand and the carafe in the other. She held out her mug and he poured the contents of the carafe into it.

He glanced at the empty carafe. "Should I make more?"

"Not unless you're staying for a second cup."

"I'm not. I have barn duty in a little bit. I just... needed to get out of the bunkhouse and my feet took me over here."

"Your feet operate independently from the rest of you?"

"Sometimes. Don't yours ever do that?"

"No, and neither do yours. Don't blame this on your feet. What's on your mind?"

"You."

"What a surprise. Not that it matters in our case, but it's supposed to be bad luck for the groom to see the bride on the day of the wedding."

"I've heard that, too. Mind if I sit down?"

"Be my guest. Help yourself to a brownie."

"Thanks. I will." Settling into the chair on her right, he put the carafe on the small table between them and picked up a brownie. He took a bite, chewed and swallowed. "I've missed these."

"I'll bring some to poker night."

"You're going to play?"

"Leo invited me. I figured it would be okay with you."

"Yes, absolutely. Glad to have you."

"Especially if I bring brownies."

"I'd be happy for you to come even if you didn't bring brownies."

"That's nice to hear. I've missed poker with you guys. Getting back to our weekly games will make things feel more like they used to. For me, at least."

He finished off his brownie and sipped his coffee. Then he looked over at her. "Do you think things will ever be the same?"

She met his gaze. "Of course not. That's impossible. People change. Attitudes change. But we can do our best and—"

"Two months ago you had a suggestion and I rejected it."

Uh-oh. She'd been one-handing her coffee, but she needed two for this discussion. She looked away and dragged in a breath. "You were right to reject it. That suggestion was all wrong for you. I understand that, now."

"Do you still want me?"

Damn. If he kept this up she'd spill her coffee for sure. She didn't dare turn her head in his direction. "That doesn't matter."

"I think it does. You can't put the toothpaste back in the tube."

Maybe she was getting hysterical, because she had to swallow a giggle. "What a romantic thing to say."

"So I don't have the right words, but the point is, we want each other and that's not going away. The more time we hang out together, the more we'll want to do something about it."

"That's why you need to find a girlfriend, buster." She gave up and put her coffee on the table before she drenched herself.

"I don't want a girlfriend. I want you."

"Stop it, Rafe." She swallowed and glanced at him. He was focused on her, his brown eyes dark and intense under the shadow of his hat. "Getting involved with me is not in your best interests. Or mine." Her heart thrummed with excitement and her rebellious body was in a hot argument with her better self. "I won't have it."

"So that's a no?" His voice was deceptively calm, at complete odds with his fierce expression.

"A no and a hell, no."

He put down his mug and stood. "Okay, but you're setting us up for major frustration."

Her jaw tightened. "*I'm* not. *You* are. You have more self-discipline than any person I know. Use it. Give up on me."

"I've tried. I can't." He touched two fingers to the brim of his hat. "See you at the altar."

15

Red was delighted when Rafe called at ten to ask if he could come over and talk to her about rings. She had several for him to choose from.

He'd never been in her house. The Brotherhood usually encountered the Babes in a group, either when they were putting on a barrel racing demonstration at Ed's arena or having a party at Henri's house.

Red lived at the end of a dirt road and her rustic cabin was nestled in a stand of pines and gold-leafed aspens. Like most everyone in the Apple Grove area, she had a front porch. Hers had a cushioned swing and dozens of potted plants.

She opened the door before he knocked. Her mass of curly hair, fire-engine red and down to her shoulders, dominated her appearance. Her outfit was something loose and flowing. Shades of purple. Nothing like the jeans, boots and Western shirt she wore for barrel racing.

Her smile took over her entire face. "I'm thrilled that you're doing this." She gestured for him to step inside. "I'll have a chance to consult with you about the vows."

"I don't have the say-so on that, ma'am. Kate would have to—"

"I'm going to Henri's at noon, so I'll get her input then. I'll just blend whatever you say and she says. It'll be fine. Perfect."

"That's quite a collection of plants you have on the porch." He took off his hat as he came through the door.

"I'll have to bring them in soon now that the nights are getting colder."

He glanced around at the jungle she had indoors. "Will they fit?"

"Oh, I'll manage to squeeze them in. I always do. Can I get you something? Coffee, herbal tea, hard cider, vodka?"

"Vodka?"

"For your nerves. People can't smell it on your breath as easily as other alcoholic beverages."

"Thanks, but I'm okay. I don't need anything."

"You're not okay, Rafe. Your aura is in big trouble. Anxiety is coming off you in waves."

He shrugged. "Goes with the territory."

"I understand. You're marrying the woman of your dreams, but she's not giving you her heart or her body."

He sucked in a breath. "You don't mess around."

"Oh, I mess around all the time. Just not with peoples' emotions. I'll put on some music with a vibration that may help calm you. I could do a Reiki session, too, if you'd like."

"I appreciate the offer, ma'am, but maybe we should see about the rings, first."

"We'll do that. I can tell that's one of your stressors, so let's get that out of the way. I can measure your finger, but do you know Kate's ring size?"

"There's a size to rings?"

"Yes."

"Kate's fingers are about half the thickness of mine. Can you figure it from there?"

"I don't think so. How about texting her?"

"I could." He'd rather not. He liked his smooth exit line this morning—*see you at the altar.* He wanted those to be the last words he said to her until she laid eyes on him as she walked down the aisle. A text exchange would dilute the drama of his parting shot.

But if he got something that was too small, he'd be stuck trying to work it onto her finger. If it was too big, she might lose it. Tucking his hat under his arm, he sent the text asking for her ring size.

She didn't respond. Was she ignoring him? Had he ticked her off so much that she'd called off the wedding? No, she couldn't. Ginny needed the money.

"Rafe, breathe."

He glanced at Red. She'd put on the music she'd talked about, some folks chanting with gongs and flutes in the background. "Thanks, ma'am, but I'm breathing."

"Not from your diaphragm. You need several deep, cleansing breaths to clear that negative energy. Like this." She demonstrated, breathing deep and making hand motions like she was trying to lift a bundle of laundry from her waist to her chin and lowering it again.

The chime of Kate's text saved him from having to imitate that routine. "She says the ring finger on her left hand is a six. She had to try on the rings everyone there was wearing to find that out. I guess they're doing the hair styling and nail painting right now."

"That sounds right. Hair and nails were this morning, then lunch, then makeup, then a short break before putting on the dresses."

"You make it sound like an all-day procedure."

"Because it is. Lucy and her bridal party went through a similar routine in April."

"I suppose they did. I didn't pay much attention. The guys just shave, shower and put on their outfits. Takes about thirty minutes, tops."

"It's different with the women. Anyway, thank goodness she was with a group and could figure out her ring size. Come on into my workshop." She led the way toward a room filled with a bewildering collection of shelves of various heights, and cabinets with drawers of every size.

Two large work tables held materials he couldn't identify and tools he didn't recognize except for the soldering iron and a mallet. Red's workshop was unlike anything he'd ever experienced. If magic existed anywhere besides in storybooks, it existed here.

"Let me have your hat."

He handed it over and she laid it brim side up on a cleared space near the end of one of the tables.

Walking to a wall lined with pegs that held twine, wire and thin strips of leather, she took down something resembling a large key ring, except it was loaded with a graduated series of metal circles instead of keys. "I'll get you measured and then we'll look for something that might help heal this fractured relationship."

"I wouldn't call it fractured." That sounded too much like an ER situation.

"Let me have your left hand." She started working her way through the set of ring measurements. "Do you like *severed relationship* better?"

He laughed. "Not when you're fooling with my fingers. I need those."

"Didn't mean to freak you out. So how would you describe the state of your relationship with Kate?"

"I'd prefer something like *light sprain* or *minor bruise*."

Her expression was loaded with sympathy. "I'm sure you would, but they're not accurate."

He sighed. "I guess not."

"For what it's worth, I've consulted my guides on this matter, and they predict a major upheaval will take place soon."

"Like what?" He wasn't fond of major upheavals. He'd already had enough to last him a while.

"They didn't give me specifics. They seldom do. They said *upheaval*, though, not *disaster*, so I tend to think this will be a blessing in disguise."

"I'm all for that."

"I've found your size. Let's look at rings." She pulled out a shallow, wide drawer from under one of the work benches.

He stayed a respectful distance behind her, but his added height allowed him an excellent view. A tray lined with black velvet-covered notches for rings fit perfectly into the drawer. Not every notch was filled, but even so, he estimated several dozen rings were stored there.

Some glittered with stones and others were bands of etched silver. "I don't know where to start."

"That's okay. I do. I don't have any gold. It's too expensive for me to work with. But silver is very Western and has a lovely spiritual component. It'll also go with—wait, I'm not supposed to mention that."

"Her dress?"

"Never mind. Focus on the task. What do you see that you like? The sixes are up here." She sketched a border in the air around a section of rings.

He pointed to a delicate band inlaid with turquoise and a green stone he couldn't name. "I like that one."

Red smiled. "Trust your instincts, Rafe. That's the one I would have chosen for Kate. The turquoise is very feminine and stimulates romantic love and friendship. It's very calming."

He'd take that with a grain of salt, but it was a pretty ring. "What about the green stone?"

"That's malachite. It opens the heart to unconditional love and encourages risk-taking and change."

"That would be a bonus."

"You sound amused. I sense you have doubts about the power of these stones."

"I'll be honest with you, Red. It seems a little far-fetched that a stone could do all that. I mean, it just sits there."

"Everything has a vibration, even stones."

"If you say so."

"Anyway, you like the ring, right?"

"I do. I'll take it."

"You don't want to know the price?"

"It doesn't matter. That's the perfect ring for Kate. She won't be able to wear it very often because of her job, but it suits her."

"I agree." She plucked it from the tray. "The wider bands are what men usually choose. Anything in that bottom quadrant should fit you."

"Is mine supposed to match hers?"

"Not necessarily. I've never been a big fan of that concept. You should pick the one that speaks to you."

He flashed her a grin. "I don't hear a thing. They're all silent as a stone."

"Very funny. It's a figure of speech."

"I like that one with the single black stone and the etching around it."

"Sure you do. I'm not the least surprised. Hematite removes negative energy and strengthens confidence. Warriors carried it in battle to help heal them from their wounds."

"Fortunately, I'm not planning to go into battle."

"That's where you're wrong. You've already been wounded. But you have amazing self-healing powers and hematite will bolster your natural abilities in that direction."

"What's the etching?"

Her eyes twinkled. "Fertility symbols."

"Oh?" Warmth rose from his collar.

"Rumor has it that you want children."

"I do, but—"

"This ring will increase your chances."

Not if he was never allowed in Kate's bed. But he wanted kids and so did she. If he could convince her that it wasn't too late... the concept made him dizzy with excitement. "I'll take it."

"Well done." She opened another drawer, lifted out a velvet pouch and dropped both rings into it.

"How much do I owe you?"

She handed him the pouch. "They're my wedding gift to you and Kate."

"Hey, no, that's not right. You labored over these and paid for the materials. I want to—"

"My reward will be watching you and Kate work this out."

"What if we don't?"

"Ah, negativity! You need that hematite desperately, Rafe. Once Kate puts that ring on your finger, don't take it off."

"Okay, I won't. And thank you." His phone pinged again. The text was from Nick, saying he was on his way to the bunkhouse with Garrett. The Brotherhood would be gathering for lunch today. "I should be going." He grabbed his hat and put it on. "Oh, wait. Didn't you want to talk about the vows?"

"I thought I did, but now that you've chosen those rings, I know exactly what I want to say."

"But you'll discuss it with Kate?"

"I will. In fact, you shouldn't take your ring since Kate needs to give it to you during the ceremony. I didn't think of that." She held out her hand. "I'll deliver it when I go to Henri's. Millie needs to be the one in charge of it."

He pulled out the hematite ring and gave it to her, although he didn't want to. What if something happened to it between now and four?

She must have seen the reluctance in his expression, because she patted his shoulder. "It'll be fine. You'll get it back this afternoon when Kate slips it on your finger."

"Right. Thanks again. I'll see you soon." He started toward her plant-filled living room.

"Wait a minute. Take this."

He turned around.

She came toward him, arm extended. A larger version of the lustrous black stone rested in her palm. "You can put it in your pocket for the rest of the day. Take it to the ceremony. Nothing wrong with having extra protection."

He reached for the stone, hesitated and withdrew his hand. "I don't need to do that. But thanks for the offer."

She sighed. "Look, I know you're a big, tough cowboy who has everything under control and thinks it's juvenile to put faith in a pebble he carries in his pocket."

He met her gaze. "I wouldn't say I have everything under control, but it's going okay. The ring is great, but I don't need—"

"Charley was fond of hematite, too."

That got him in the solar plexus. He swallowed. "I didn't know that."

"He told me it fascinated him, that it looked like a liquid turned solid. He almost expected it to melt in his hand. I gave him a stone to carry around and Henri said it was almost always in his pocket. Now she carries it."

"No kidding."

"She also has a tiger's eye I gave her that's about this size. It's a stone that helps us see things clearly and act with courage."

"That's Henri, all right, but she's just naturally clear-thinking and brave."

"And you're just naturally strong and resistant to negativity. But in times of trouble, it doesn't hurt to have an extra source of power."

He took the stone and rubbed his thumb over the smooth surface. "It does look as if it could melt."

"But it won't. It'll work hard for you, absorbing any negative energy coming your way."

He smiled. "Thanks, Red. Charley was one of the happiest guys I've ever known. Guess I can't go wrong carrying the stone he liked."

"That's for sure. I wish you happiness, Rafe."

"I'm working on it." On impulse, he gave her a quick kiss on the cheek. Then he tucked the stone in his pocket and left. If it was good enough for Charley Fox, it was good enough for him.

<u>16</u>

Henri's living room had been turned into a beauty parlor for the day, and Kate loved the sparkles Eva had put in her hair. She was less enamored of the manicure routine.

She'd smeared two of her nails within a minute of Eva completing the job. While Eva worked to repair those, Kate grabbed a tissue to blow her nose and accidentally messed up a nail on the other hand.

"Ack! Sorry, Eva. I'm so not used to this."

"Never mind. I'll fix that one, too."

Ed came by to check out the situation. "You probably should have gone with shellac, sweetie."

"She doesn't like the smell," Eva said.

"Nobody does," Millie called over from the straight-backed chair where Josette was working on her up-do. "I'm thrilled that Kate went with regular polish."

Ed waved a dismissive hand. "The smell's temporary. And when you're done it wears like iron."

"But I don't want it to wear like iron." Kate did her best to hold still while Eva carefully recreated the French manicure on her little finger.

"It'll be gone by Monday when I go back to my regularly scheduled program in the dining hall kitchen."

"Then let us do things for you." Ed hovered near the manicure table. "Don't try to use your hands until your nails are really dry. Is there anything I can get for you right now? Some water? Coffee? Champagne?"

Kate laughed. "You keep pushing that champagne, and I'm very grateful that you brought all those bottles, but if I start now, Henri will need to roll me up to the altar in a wheelbarrow."

"Go ahead and have some if you think you can hold the flute without ruining your nails," Millie said. "I just took a glass. We'll have lunch soon and that'll soak up the booze."

"Did I hear booze? I'm in." Red swept through the front door looking like a mythic goddess in her flowing white outfit, her hair in a wild topknot and a glittery headband decorating her forehead. Silver discs hung from her earlobes and a belt of the same disks circled her hips.

Henri walked in from the kitchen, took one look at Red and let out a whoop. "Red's gone full-on high priestess! I love it!"

"Glad you approve." She twirled in the center of the room before gliding over to Kate. "Katherine, I bring you Rafael's ring." Pulling a velvet pouch from her bodice, she laid it on the manicure tray.

"Thank you, Red." Kate smiled. "Or should I call you Anastasia today?"

"Now that you mention it, I did get up on the Anastasia side of the bed this morning."

"Then Anastasia it is. Ed, could I please have a glass of champagne, after all? I think I need it to get into the spirit of this wedding."

"Oh, it'll be spirited, all right." Ed pulled a magnum out of the ice bucket and poured Kate's champagne. Strolling over with the flute in hand, she surveyed Red's outfit. "This getup's more dramatic than the last one. I might have to find me a husband just so I can have you perform the ceremony."

"Please do. I'd forgotten how much I love this role."

Kate glanced at the velvet pouch. "Would someone please take out Rafe's ring so I can see it? I'm not touching anything for the next hour except the stem of this champagne flute."

Eva capped the bottle of topcoat. "I will. I'm dying to see it."

"Me, too." Henri came over.

Loosening the top of the pouch, Eva tipped the ring into her hand. "Ooo, nice." She held it out so everyone who'd gathered around could see.

Kate's breath caught. The wide silver band with the gleaming black stone created a visceral reaction that shocked the hell out of her. It was so... *masculine.* Rafe's hands were big and very strong. But gentle, too. This afternoon she'd slide this ring on his finger. *With this ring, I thee wed.*

Henri peered at her. "Do you like it?"

"I do. It looks just like him."

"I know what you mean. I don't think he's ever worn a ring before. But I can picture him wearing this one."

She could, too. But would he? Or would he take it off tonight and tuck it away somewhere before he went to bed? Alone. In the bunkhouse. On their wedding night.

"Hematite's perfect for a guy," Eva said. "Very sexy." She examined it more closely. "What's etched on the sides, Red?"

"Fertility symbols."

Kate's head snapped up and her gaze met Red's. "Does he know that?"

"He does."

"And he chose it anyway?"

"Yep." Red exchanged a glance with Henri.

Kate gulped. "Does mine have—"

"No. Yours is completely different. Different stones, different design, no symbols. Well, the ring itself is a symbol, of course."

"Of course. I'm… I think it's probably better if our rings don't match, though. I mean, under the circumstances."

"That would have been impossible. I never make the same design twice."

"Well, this one is beautiful." And scary. What was he thinking, choosing a ring that celebrated procreation? His decision alarmed her. And—to be honest—excited her. She took a hefty swallow of champagne.

"I'll need to take that ring at some point," Millie said. "I haven't figured out how to keep from losing it or forgetting it. Henri, you were put in charge of Matt's ring for Lucy's wedding. How did you keep track of it?"

"I don't remember."

Kate rolled her eyes. "You two aren't exactly inspiring confidence."

"I'm kidding," Henri said. "I know exactly what I did. I kept it inside my bra until right before I walked down the aisle. Then I took it out and put it on my thumb until I had to give it to Lucy."

"Yes, you sure did," Lucy called from the kitchen. She came to the doorway, wiping her hands on a towel. "That bra and thumb routine was nerve-wracking. I just knew you'd forget to take it out and you'd end up fishing in your bra while we were standing at the altar."

"But the point is, I didn't forget. And Millie won't, either, because I'll be right there before she starts down the aisle and I'll remind her."

"I feel slightly better, now." Kate polished off her champagne.

"Have another glass of champagne and you'll feel on top of the world." Ed took her flute.

"I believe you, but first I want to confer with Red-slash-Anastasia about the vows. Did you discuss them with Rafe?"

"A little."

"Did he have anything he wanted said? Not that it matters, I guess, but—"

"He trusts me to say the right things."

"Like what?"

"The food is ready!" Pam came to the kitchen door. "Time for all you lovely ladies to have a seat at the dining table while Peggy, Lucy and I serve you the most amazing lunch you'll have today."

Kate glanced at her fingernails. "I wonder if I should have someone feed me."

"I'll do it." Isabel pushed herself up from the sofa. "I'm one of the few sober ones here and I can use the practice before Cleo Marie's born."

"I was sort of kidding," Kate said. "I'm sure I can at least—"

"Let her feed you, girlfriend," Eva said. "The time for making repairs is getting shorter and shorter."

"Oh, yeah, definitely feed her, Isabel." Millie sounded gleeful at the prospect. "So Ed can take pictures."

<u>17</u>

Saturday's usual schedule had been adjusted to allow time for wedding preparation and the ceremony itself. Other than early morning barn duty, Rafe had the day off. Henri had also rescheduled the afternoon trail rides and hired Ed's wrangler Teague to handle the evening barn chores.

The Brotherhood's time was freed up and Rafe needed every single one of those guys around him today. Garrett and Jake prepared what looked like a great lunch, although he didn't eat much and couldn't taste what he did eat. Nobody commented on his lack of appetite.

The wedding wasn't discussed, either, for which he was grateful. Instead, reminiscing over bottles of cider seemed to be the order of the day. Since Garrett hadn't been at the Buckskin long, he couldn't reminisce. He was a champion listener, though. And an appreciative audience.

Eventually, inevitably, Nick's phone alarm chimed. He glanced across the battered dining table at Rafe. "Time for us to get cleaned up and into our duds, bro, since we need to be there ahead of these jokers."

"Yep." His stomach clenched.

"That silver brocade vest is stylin'," Leo said.

"What vest?"

"The one you'll be wearing today. You didn't check out what's in the garment bag?"

"Nope." He'd hung it in the small closet at the far end of the bunkroom yesterday afternoon and hadn't touched it since.

"Hope you don't mind that I looked."

"Not at all. It's just clothes."

"I was curious if it would be the same outfits we wore for Matt and Lucy's wedding. They're the same, except for the vest."

"Silver, huh?" The velvet pouch holding Kate's ring had been in his jeans pocket, along with the hematite, ever since he'd left Red's house. Red had started to say the silver ring would match something. Likely his vest had been chosen to match something, too. Kate's dress would have silver in it.

A lot of folks were putting in plenty of effort to make this event nice. He'd rather take a whipping than go through with it, but he'd promised, and Kate was counting on him. He stood. "Let's do it."

He left the kitchen, Nick right behind him. "I probably should have checked to make sure the sizes were right."

Nick laughed. "Yeah, it's a little late to worry about that now."

"The tux shop kept our measurements from last time, so they should fit, but might as well look before we hit the showers." He opened the closet door, hauled out the garment bag and twisted the hangers so he could hook it over the top of the door.

"Did Matt have a vest? I don't remember a vest."

"I don't think he had one." He unzipped the garment bag. "But Henri's in charge this time and I'll bet she wants to show Kate's aunt a thing or two. If I'm right and Kate's dress has silver in it, then we'll look coordinated."

"How do you know about Kate's dress? I thought that was a closely guarded secret."

"When I got the rings from Red, she let something slip."

"Speaking of Kate's ring, where is it? I'm supposed to keep it for you until the critical moment in the ceremony."

"Right here." He reached in his pocket and pulled out the velvet pouch. "I don't know if you should keep it in here or what."

"I asked Matt how Seth handled it. Seth kept Lucy's ring in his pocket, but that makes me nervous."

"Yeah, me, too. You could keep it in the pouch, I guess."

"But then I'm fumbling around with the pouch and I could drop it. We'll be standing in the grass, too, so it could get lost in the grass, or fall into a gopher hole, or—"

"A squirrel could come romping by and steal it." Rafe grinned. Good to know he hadn't entirely lost his sense of humor. "Could we possibly be overthinking this?"

"I have an idea. Let me see it."

"Okay." He opened the pouch and dumped it into his hand.

"Hey, that's pretty, bro." Nick picked it up carefully. "I recognize the turquoise, but what's the green one?"

"Malachite."

"I've heard of that, now that you say it. Anyway, what if I put it on my pinky finger?" He slid it on. "It fits and I won't lose it that way."

"You're gonna wear it from now until the ceremony?"

"No, that's a bad idea. Since we'll all be at Henri's place, I might accidentally let someone see it, and nobody should see it before Kate does. I could keep it in the pouch in my pocket and put it on my pinky finger once we're at the altar waiting for Millie."

"That could work."

He turned the ring so it caught the light. "I wonder if Eva would like a ring like this. Everybody talks about diamonds, but this is cool. Was it expensive?"

"I don't know. Red wouldn't let me pay for it. Or mine."

"That sounds like her. Maybe she needs something done around her house."

"I thought of that. When this is all over, I'll see if she has any jobs she needs handled."

"Perfect." Nick handed back the ring. "Kate will like it."

"Even if she does, she doesn't wear rings."

"I predict she'll wear this one."

"And I predict she won't. Even if she normally wore them, which she doesn't, it's a wedding ring and she hates that idea."

Nick gazed at him. "Then sometime, like maybe at the party tonight, tell her it's a friendship ring. She can't hate that idea. And you're being a hell of a friend."

He took a deep breath. "So are you, Nicholas. So are you."

* * *

As instructed by Henri, Nick drove Rafe over to her place thirty minutes before the ceremony. Eva was waiting on the front porch when they pulled up.

She came down the steps to meet them. "I've been assigned to escort you two handsome gentlemen upstairs to one of Henri's spare rooms until we're ready for you."

"Are you having problems?" Nick glanced toward the backyard. "Because if you're having problems, I'd be glad to—"

"Everything's fine. We're just putting the final touches on the arched trellis. It's under control. Your job is to keep Rafe calm and relaxed."

"Okay."

"I'm calm and relaxed." Or so he'd been telling himself. He shoved his hand in the pocket of his Western-cut tux pants to make sure the hematite was still there.

Nick gave him a quick once-over, as if trying to judge his condition. "Maybe we should just wait in the truck, sweetheart. I don't think sitting in one of Henri's spare rooms is going to help my brother relax."

"I put a couple of cold bottles of cider up there. And a deck of cards."

"That was thoughtful." Nick turned to him. "You tell me, bro. Want to go hang out in one of Henri's spare rooms, drink cider and play cards?"

"Can't say I do. I haven't eaten much today and I've already had plenty of cider. I don't think drinking more is a good idea."

Eva looked distressed. "I could get you a sandwich if that would help."

"No, thanks, ma'am. I appreciate the trouble you've gone to, but—"

"It's no trouble, Rafe. What you're doing is… above and beyond. Leaving you to sit out here in Nick's truck doesn't seem right."

"I'm rather fond of Nicholas's truck. We go back a long way."

Nick smiled. "She has a few miles on her, but she gets me where I need to go."

"Mostly. Unless you leave the lights on and I have to give you a jump in the middle of the night." He winked at Eva, who had been involved in that debacle.

"Well, it's broad daylight now, so no worries." Nick turned back to Eva. "We'll wait in my truck. Just come get us when you're ready. We can go straight from here to the backyard."

"Want me to bring you some water?"

"Not for me," Nick said, "but if Rafe—"

"No, thanks. Might spill it on my outfit."

"All right, then." She patted Nick's chest. "You look amazing. You, too, Rafe. Nice vest. I'll go tell Henri you're staying out here." She climbed the steps to the porch, her skirt swishing around her knees.

"Thanks again, sweetheart!"

"You're welcome!"

Deep in his Eva trance, Nick watched her cross the porch. Rafe got a kick out of the guy. In this condition, Nick was oblivious to everything but the woman of his dreams. Poor lovesick slob.

When she went through the door, he snapped out of it. "Sorry. It's just—"

"I know." Rafe smiled. "I'm happy for you."

"And the great thing is, I believe you are happy for me. You don't do envy."

"Sure, I do. I envy you and Leo because you're both younger than me and your sperm has greater motility than mine."

"What?"

Just the sort of reaction he was looking for. Perfect topic to keep them distracted. "I'll tell you once we're in the truck. You need privacy for a subject like that." They were still hotly debating the issue when Eva walked down the porch steps again.

Until that moment, his reason for being here had slipped into the background, overshadowed by the riveting topic of sperm speed. The truck cab had become a comforting and familiar refuge.

But when Eva reappeared, his heart shifted into high gear and breathing became a chore.

"Looks like they're ready for us." Nick reached a hand over the console, forearm up and palm out. "Good luck, bro."

Rafe grasped his hand. "Couldn't do this without you, Nicholas."

"Wouldn't let you." Nick had a grip like iron. When he put his heart into it, he could cause pain.

Fine with Rafe. His brother was communicating loyalty and love. He squeezed hard, too, and let go.

Taking a ragged breath, he exited the truck and stepped back into reality. Was that CJ playing or a recording? Yeah, it was CJ, strumming his guitar, creating ambiance.

Eva escorted them around the house to the backyard. She chatted with Nick, but Rafe's rapid heartbeat and tortured breathing temporarily deafened him.

Henri's backyard had been transformed into a simple wedding venue. An arched trellis decorated with fall leaves and mums stood at the far side and white wedding bells dangled from several wires strung between the house and the trees at the edge of the yard.

CJ sat on a bar stool off to one side of the trellis. Three short rows of white folding chairs were set up with an aisle down the middle.

His brothers were already seated in the chairs. They must have driven up and hiked back here while he was engrossed in his conversation with Nick. The Babes were here, minus Henri. Isabel was with them. Ben, too.

Ed roamed the area with her video camera in her hand and her regular one on a strap around her neck. Red stood by the arched trellis, eyes closed, maybe listening to her guides. Henri would be in the house with Kate and Millie, waiting for their cue.

Damn, his chest hurt. Red would tell him to breathe, but he was afraid if he tried to suck in more air he'd start coughing. That hematite in his pocket was supposed to help in situations like this. Time for it to kick in. Past time.

CJ looked up, caught sight of Rafe and Nick walking in and switched gears. The gentle melody gave way to the intro for Keith Urban's lively *Somebody Like You* and CJ began to sing.

The mood of the gathering swung from mellow to joyful. Red's eyes popped open. She glanced his way and sent him one of her mega-watt smiles.

Rafe's chest pain eased with every note of CJ's happy tune. He was getting *married*, damn it. Kate had chosen him for this adventure, not some other schmuck, and he'd view it as a positive step on their journey.

As he took his place with Nick by his side, CJ moved into his next tune, Kelsea Ballerini's *Unapologetically.* No telling who'd decided on these songs. Music was another thing he and Kate hadn't discussed. Whoever had been put in charge of it, he approved of the choices.

Millie stepped out of the back door of Henri's house and came down the porch steps. Her copper-colored hair was piled in a fancy arrangement on top of her head and she wore the same leaf-green dress she'd had for Lucy and Matt's spring wedding.

Her bouquet of yellow and orange mums plucked from Henri's yard signaled fall. She executed a cute little dance step as she moved toward them. Nick gave her a subtle thumbs-up.

She returned the gesture, and Rafe's silver and hematite ring caught the light. He choked back a laugh. She'd put it on her thumb.

Nick leaned toward him. "Great minds."

"Kate's is on your pinky?"

"Yes, sir, safe and sound."

Once Millie was in position, CJ changed the tempo to something slower, a gentle waltz. He began to sing *I Won't Let Go* by Rascal Flatts. Had CJ picked it? Kate? If Rafe could have chosen one song to tell her what he wanted to say, this would be it.

As the music gained momentum, she appeared, a vision in a silvery, fluid dress with a skirt cut to reveal her white boots stitched in silver. Sparkles in her golden hair completed the effect. An angel.

He gulped. He'd promised not to lose it, but dear God, she was incredible. He ached for this woman. And this song, filled with all the unspoken words in his bruised heart... it was almost enough to break him.

Everyone stood and turned in her direction. Looping her arm through Henri's, she grasped her bouquet of mums in both hands, trained her gaze on him, and started forward.

Henri gave him an encouraging smile, but Kate's mouth was set in a grim line. She looked neither right nor left. Her gray eyes focused on him with laser-like intensity. The closer she came, the more resolute her expression. Her throat moved in a slow swallow.

He held out his hand. Henri took Kate's bouquet and stepped back. Kate hesitated. Then she came to him. He gripped her trembling hand with all the love in his heart and gently coaxed her to stand at his side.

Weaving his fingers through hers, he held on as Red began to speak. Kate shivered.

"It'll be okay," he murmured and squeezed her hand.

She gave a quick nod. "I know." And she squeezed back.

<u>18</u>

She'd been tempted to turn around. The scene was totally different from her first wedding, but all the elements were there. Just pared down.

What had been somewhat reasonable this morning had looked completely insane now. Maybe she could get Ginny's money another way. Her cottage wasn't that far. Given the element of surprise, she could have been inside with the doors locked before anyone could catch her.

Then Rafe had held out his hand. His big, strong, incredibly gentle hand. Once she'd connected with his strength and resolve, she'd gathered her forces. Her friends had worked hard to make this happen. She wouldn't let them down.

If any other man had waited at the end of that endless aisle, she wouldn't have made it. But Rafe had promised to stand beside her today and his word was his bond. He would do everything in his power to keep them on course. They were doing the right thing... for Ginny.

Gradually her panic subsided long enough for Red's words to filter through.

"True love is a circle—infinite and unconditional. No beginning and no end. And to represent that here today, I'm asking that you all leave your chairs, move them if you need to, and form a circle around this couple."

Kate blinked and glanced at Rafe. "Did you—"

He shook his head.

Red lowered her voice. "Just go with it, kids." She looked at Millie and Nick. "You two join hands behind me and link up with the first to come forward."

As everyone left their seats, CJ started singing *The Circle of Life.*

Red grinned. "I didn't tell him to do that, but it works."

Because the group wasn't large, they created the circle quickly. Somebody muttered *musical chairs, anyone?* It sounded like Jake. Kate smiled. Count on Jake to provide comic relief.

CJ stopped playing, put down his guitar and found a place between Isabel and Garrett.

Red looked around. "Perfect. A perfect circle, with no beginning and no end. A circle of love and protection. A circle of caring for one another that has no beginning and will have no end."

Tears of gratitude pushed at the back of Kate's eyes. She'd vowed not to cry during this ceremony, but she hadn't been prepared for this gesture of solidarity. Having her best friends literally circling the wagons hit her right where she lived.

"Bless this circle." Red lifted her arms. "Bless the loyal friends creating it and bless Rafael and Katherine, who stand within it, safe and surrounded by unconditional love."

Rafe's grip tightened. She held onto him for dear life, too, as tears dribbled down her cheeks.

"We will conclude this ceremony with the symbol of infinite and unending love as Katherine and Rafael exchange rings." She lowered her voice. "Who wants to go first?"

Rafe's voice was husky but firm. "I will." He turned to Nick, who handed him a ring before Kate got a look at it.

"Rafael, place the ring on Katherine's finger and look into her eyes."

Kate tried hard to keep her hand from shaking as she held it out. Rafe cupped it gently in his as he slid the ring on her finger. The delicate circle of silver was warm. And stunning. The beauty of the turquoise and malachite stones made her gasp with pleasure.

"Look up at me," he murmured.

Heart racing, she lifted her gaze to his... and forgot to breathe. *Love.* If he'd tried to hide it before, he'd given up. He was letting her see everything in his heart. He was so much braver than she was.

"Rafael Banner, do you promise to honor Katherine from this day forward, share both her pain and joy, shelter her in the circle of your arms, rejoice in her free will, and love her more with every passing day?"

"I do." The glow in his eyes intensified.

Red touched her shoulder. "Your turn."

She forced herself to break eye contact so she could take the ring from Millie. Rafe held out his hand, ruggedly beautiful with his neatly clipped nails, the scar on his thumb, the sprinkling of sun-bleached hair across his tan skin.

Clumsiness from an attack of nerves sabotaged her. She had trouble working the ring over his knuckle, but eventually it slipped into place. She glanced up, caught his soft smile and the light in his eyes.

"Katherine Gifford, do you promise to honor Rafe from this day forward, share both his pain and joy, shelter him in the circle of your arms, rejoice in his free will, and love him more with every passing day?"

Butterflies fluttered in her stomach as she held Rafe's gaze. She'd never talked with Red about the wording of the ceremony. Too late, now.

Only one part of that vow made her nervous. Maybe she could interpret *shelter him in the circle of her arms* as a metaphor for giving him tons of emotional support. She was certainly willing to do that. No danger there. Okay, she could go with the wording.

"Kate?"

She took a deep breath. "I do."

A sigh went up from the group.

"As a final pledge of your shared love, Rafe, will you kiss Kate?"

"Yes, I will."

Oh, right. The kiss. For the video. Then it would be done. She'd send the pictures and video to Aunt Lilith and seal the deal.

Rafe cupped her face in both hands. The wide silver band on his left ring finger brushed her cheek. Tilting her head up, he lowered his.

The pressure of his lips against hers sent a jolt of recognition straight to her core. Two long months had passed since he'd kissed her. Her body acted as if it had been two hours.

Instantly her blood heated and she began to quiver with anticipation. No! She couldn't react this way!

Shifting the angle, he dipped his tongue into her mouth. How had that happened? Had she let him in? Had she *invited* him in? Good grief, this was *not* supposed to be a hot kiss!

And what was that noise? Clapping and cheering? What the hell?

He ended the kiss as slowly as he'd begun. Lifting his head, he gazed down at her with a smile.

She couldn't seem to breathe right and she was warm all over, including her cheeks, which meant she was blushing for all the world to see.

Sure enough, the guests were enjoying the heck out of the show. A couple of the guys had added whistles to the laughter and applause. CJ had grabbed his guitar and was singing Tim McGraw's *I Like, I Love It.*

Rafe released her and his smile widened. "You'll need to let go of my vest."

She glanced down. With a cry of dismay, she released the silver brocade she'd clutched in both hands. She backed away and avoided his gaze. "I... I didn't mean to—"

"I know. That's what makes it special."

"I... um, we should—"

"Kate." Henri's voice sounded strangely tense considering the general hilarity of the group.

Still dazed, she turned in Henri's direction. "What?"

Henri tilted her head toward the side of the yard. "Do you know who that is?"

She looked beyond the circle of her friends. At the edge of the yard stood a woman in a tailored ivory suit that showed off a trim figure. Her blond hair fell to her shoulders in gentle waves.

Large sunglasses covered her eyes and her lipstick was stoplight red, visible even from here. A tan cashmere coat was draped over one arm and a gold-toned leather shoulder bag was tucked against her side. Her four-inch heels matched the bag.

A chill ran up Kate's spine. "Aunt Lilith's here."

19

Rafe gave the woman a quick glance before returning his attention to Kate, who looked stricken. "That's your Aunt Lilith?"

She nodded.

"How old is she?"

"Henri's age." She dragged in a shaky breath. "I'll bring her over."

"I'll go with you." No way was he letting her face this woman alone.

"So will I." Henri threw back her shoulders.

Rafe was worried about how Kate would take this turn of events, but at least she had Henri. He ducked his head to hide a grin as Henri charged forward, ready for battle. She damn near beat Kate over there.

Lilith's red mouth curved into a smug smile. "Hello, kitten."

Kitten? Rafe bristled. Kate was a full-grown, responsible woman, not a baby cat.

The stiletto heels gave Lilith an advantage, but Kate stood very straight and lifted her chin. "This better be a secret trip. If you told my mother you were coming here, I'll—"

"Oh, this is totally our little secret." Her aunt waved a hand, displaying long, gold-toned fingernails. "Just between you and me, kitten. Your mother and sister won't ever—"

"Henrietta Fox." Henri stuck out her hand. "Welcome to the Buckskin Ranch." Henri didn't have four-inch heels but she didn't need them. She still had a height advantage on the intruder.

"Lilith Cutler, Henrietta. Delightful to meet you."

Rafe stepped up beside Kate and slipped his hand around her waist. She was shaking, but it was subtle. He tucked her in close and her tremors eased.

She slid her arm under his Western-cut jacket. "Rafe, this is my aunt, Lilith Cutler. Aunt Lilith, I'd like you to meet my husband, Rafael Banner."

Husband. She hadn't hesitated. "Pleased to meet you, ma'am." That whopper should make his nose grow.

"I'm *very* pleased to meet you, Mr. Banner." Her calculating gaze assessed him as if he were on display in a store window. She gave a quick nod. "You'll do nicely." She turned to Henri. "I really appreciate the effort you've made for my niece. It appears you've thrown together a cute little ceremony for her."

Henri smiled, but her eyes held the gleam of cold steel. Her tone was deceptively conversational. "And it appears you've crashed it."

Go, Henri. Rafe coughed into his hand to cover a laugh.

A faint pink flush appeared on Lilith's taut cheeks, but she recovered quickly. "So I did, but I brought two cases of Dom Perignon for the reception, so I hope I'll be forgiven."

"How thoughtful of you." Butter wouldn't melt in Henri's mouth. "I think we have enough champagne, but if not, we can fill in with what you brought." She glanced over her shoulder. "Ed, how's our supply of Cristal holding up?"

"Oh, we have several magnums left, Henri."

Rafe looked behind him. The Brotherhood and the Babes had arranged themselves in a semicircle a couple of yards away, available if needed.

Lilith's flush deepened. "You have *Cristal*?"

"It's our favorite around these parts." Ed emphasized her country drawl as she walked up to stand shoulder-to-shoulder with Henri. "But if we should run out, folks'll be too pie-eyed to notice we switched to something cheaper." She extended her hand. "Edna Jane Vidal. Pleasure to meet you."

"Um, yes. Same here." Lilith gave Ed's hand a quick shake before her attention shifted warily to the group in the background. "I'm sure you're all eager to start the reception, but I'd like to get settled before I join you. My driver had to park down below, in front of that little cottage. He couldn't maneuver up here with all the trucks in the way. I understand you have some rustic cabins for rent?"

"Not presently," Henri said. "We're battling an infestation of bedbugs."

Lilith recoiled in horror. "Bedbugs?"

"A few cabins were spared and those are occupied. But you can stay with me."

"Oh, I wouldn't want to impose."

"It's your only option, I'm afraid. The Apple Grove Hotel is closed for renovations." She turned around. "Jake and Nick, would you please fetch our guest's luggage and take it up to the blue room? Matt, you and Garrett can bring up the cases of champagne."

With a chorus of *yes, ma'ams*, Rafe's brothers stepped forward.

"I'll go down to the car with you boys." Lilith adjusted the strap of her shoulder purse, which had a scaly look to it, probably alligator. "My bags are Louis Vuitton."

"I'm so glad you mentioned that, ma'am," Jake said. "Expensive, are they?"

"Very."

"Then if you would please hold my hat, I'd be much obliged." He took off his dress Stetson and handed it to her.

"Why do you need me to hold your hat?" She examined it with obvious interest.

"I intend to balance your expensive looey futon on my head like those porters in a safari. Nicholas here will do the same. He's conveniently hatless because he's a member of the wedding party, which was a no-hat situation."

"Just so my bags don't get dragged around in the dirt."

"Rest assured they will not."

"I recognize the Stetson brand. This seems to be a good quality hat."

"Yes, ma'am."

She put it on. "What do you think?"

"It's you."

"Oh, I don't know about that, but it does keep the sun off my face."

"Hey, Matt." Ed held up her camcorder as she walked toward the top of the slope. "Will you and Garrett be balancing those cases of Dom on your heads when you climb the hill?"

"I think not."

"Too bad. It would make a better video if you did."

Lucy gave Matt a nudge. "I'll hold your hat, cowboy. Yours, too, Garrett."

Aunt Lilith stared at them as if they were creatures from another planet. "Those cases weigh almost fifty pounds. I wouldn't recommend—"

"Fifty pounds? Is that all?" Matt took off his hat and gave it to Lucy. "Roll 'em, Ed." As she started her video, he turned and waved at her before heading down the hill toward the long black limo parked in front of Kate's cottage.

Garrett laughed and handed over his hat before following Matt.

Jake took Lilith's elbow. "Garrett and I will see that you get down the hill safely, ma'am."

She shook him off and lifted her chin. "Thank you, but I can manage. I made it up here on my own."

The rest of the group came over to watch as Ed filmed Lilith tottering down the hill on her stilettos, Jake and Garrett close behind. When they were standing by the limo, Ed switched off her camcorder. "Okay, you can talk now. I'll let you know when I start filming again."

"If we have a break in the action, we should take care of one tiny detail." Red held up the marriage license and a pen. "I ducked into the house to get this. It's my duty to see that it's signed."

Rafe glanced at her. "I'm glad you're on it, Red. Should we take this back inside, so we have a surface for—"

"I have a surface." CJ walked over, turned his guitar upside down and held it out. "Your surface."

"Perfect, bro. Kate? You ready?" He held out the pen.

She took a deep breath. "Sure." Grabbing the pen, she placed the license on the back of the guitar, quickly scribbled her name and handed him the pen.

He signed fast, too. She wouldn't like this part. Might as well get it over with.

Red signed her name and turned to the group. "I need two witnesses."

"I will." Henri stepped up and added her bold signature.

"I'll be the other one." Millie signed with a flourish.

"Excellent." Red took the license and pen. "I'll put this in the house for now."

"Hey, Henri." Millie looked over at her. "Why'd you tell Kate's aunt we had bedbugs? What's that all about?"

"I don't get that, either," Rafe said. "Why don't you want her in one of the cabins?"

"Because Charley always said to keep your friends close and your enemies closer. I don't trust that woman any farther than I can throw her."

Ed's expression brightened. "It would be fun to try it, though, just to see how far she'd fly. Bet I could grab her by her skinny arm, whip her around and launch her like a javelin."

"Yeah, that would be fun." Henri let out a resigned sigh. "But no matter how much she annoys us, we have to be careful." She glanced at Kate. "I won't allow her to run the show or insult anyone, but I don't want to tick her off so much that she calls off your deal."

"I don't think she will, but—"

"Is she a woman of her word?"

"Amazingly enough, she always has been. I'd say our ace in the hole is Rafe. She's clearly pleased with my choice." She looked up at him. "She can brag to her friends about the ruggedly handsome cowboy I found out West."

Nice to hear, although it made him blush. "Just so I don't have to turn into a suck-up. I'd hate that on general principles, and even more in this case."

"I don't think that's necessary," Henri said. "But you've probably figured out what is required now that she's here."

He had, but he didn't want to be the first to say it.

"Rafe and I will work this out." Kate turned to him, a plea in her gray eyes. "It won't be a problem."

"No, it won't be a problem." He wasn't going to disagree with her in front of everyone. But yeah, it would be a problem. This was their wedding night. Now they'd have to spend it together.

20

Don't panic. Take it one step at a time. Great self-talk. It wasn't working. Kate's anxiety level was sky-high. Rafe had backed up her statement to keep the peace. But his gaze had sent a very different message.

Aunt Lilith was no dummy. If Rafe spent his nights in the bunkhouse, she'd figure out the marriage was an elaborate scheme. He'd have to sleep in the cottage. Kate had a plan, but now wasn't the time to discuss it.

The limo drove away and Ed signaled that she was filming again as the safari started back up the hill. Aunt Lilith took the lead wearing Jake's Stetson. She looked good in it, but she looked good in anything.

Jake and Nick balanced gold-toned leather suitcases on their heads and followed behind. Nick had a matching carry-on hanging from his shoulder. Matt and Garrett brought up the rear with the cases of champagne.

CJ brought over his guitar and launched into *The Lion Sleeps Tonight.* Everybody joined in on the chant and CJ managed a decent falsetto on the lyrics. Aunt Lilith glanced up once, shook her head, and kept going.

When she topped the rise, Henri motioned her toward the house and led her inside, followed by her porters. CJ finished up with a flourish.

Ed turned off the camcorder. "That's a wrap! Thank you all for the soundtrack. Who's helping me load those folding chairs into the back of my truck? I'm taking them over to the fire pit so we'll have enough chairs."

"I'm on it," Leo said.

Kate glanced up at Rafe. "I should go change."

"You look terrific in that dress." His gaze warmed. "Great choice."

"Thank you." Awareness fluttered its wings. "The vest looks good on you, too."

"I'm glad you like it. It's too tight. I'm ready to ditch the thing." He pulled on the end of his string tie and it came undone. "Once Nick's delivered that suitcase upstairs, he and I should take off."

"I'll hang out with you until he comes back."

He smiled. "Thanks. Your aunt isn't anything like I pictured her. Why does she look so young?"

"Cosmetic surgery. She does a lot of it. She refuses to age past forty-five."

"Why?"

"I don't know. You could ask her."

"No, thanks." Once the string tie was loose, he unfastened the top two buttons of his white tux shirt, revealing a tanned column of his throat. "I plan to spend as little time with her as I can get away with."

"Me, too." His mini-strip was riveting. Not good.

"But you're her niece." He ran his finger around the inside of the collar. "Won't she expect to hang out with you?"

"She's never wanted to before." If she asked him to stop fooling with his clothes, that could lead to a discussion she wasn't ready to have.

"Then why's she here?"

"Curiosity. Making a dramatic entrance. To my knowledge she's never been out West. It'll be an exotic adventure to share with her friends. You notice how she latched onto Jake's hat."

"That's it? Curiosity?"

"Also, she trusts no one. She's making sure I'm not trying to put one over on her."

"Which you are, kitten."

"I *hate* when she calls me that."

"I hate it more. It reduces you to a vulnerable little creature. Cute, playful, clueless."

"She's done it ever since I can remember. When I was young I didn't care so much. But now..."

"If you think it's worth it, you could ask her not to call you that."

"I could. Maybe it doesn't matter."

"And maybe it does." He unbuttoned his vest and sighed in relief. "I'll sure be glad to get rid of these clothes. They don't breathe worth a damn."

He likely had no idea how his actions were affecting her. Standing there with his collar open, his string tie hanging loose and his vest unbuttoned, he looked like a cover model for a romance novel.

The vest was too tight because he had such a muscular chest. The tux shirt was snug, too, stretched by his magnificent—

"Hey." His voice had taken on that husky tone again.

"What?" She glanced up.

"I'm only human. If you're going to look at me like that, I—"

"You're the one who's getting undressed right in front of me." She lowered her voice. "I'm only human, too."

"Oh. I was just... I didn't realize..." He blew out a breath. "We need to talk."

"I know, but—"

"There are my two lovebirds!" Aunt Lilith hurried down the back steps, a turquoise gift bag in one hand. Tiffany blue. It was a little large for jewelry, a little small for crystal goblets. Definitely a wedding gift from her aunt's favorite store.

"Henri told me you'd specified no gifts, which is proper for a second wedding, but I couldn't resist bringing you something." She handed it to Kate. "I wanted you to open it before we go over to the ring of fire, or whatever you call it."

Ring of fire sounded about right. "Thank you so much, but you really didn't need—"

"Yes, I absolutely did. You'll see why when you open it."

Kate pulled out a turquoise box and set the bag on the grass. Then she opened the lid. At first she couldn't identify the silver object lying on white satin. Then she did.

Rafe peered into the box. "What is it?"

"A rattle." Kate fought the impulse to pick it up and heave it as far as she could. "A silver rattle from Tiffany's."

"Oh." He packed a world of meaning into that single syllable.

"Isn't it precious?" Aunt Lilith plucked it out of the box and turned it this way and that so it gleamed in the afternoon sun. "I couldn't resist it."

Rafe's troubled gaze caught and held Kate's as he silently mouthed *I'm sorry.*

Her aunt was oblivious, focused, as usual, on herself. "Now you know my dirty little secret, the real reason I wanted you to get married. My friends all have grandchildren. We call ourselves the Nifty Nanas, which is fun because we don't look anything like grandmothers are supposed to look."

The blood rushed in Kate's ears. It hurt to breathe. "Is this... a condition of the money? Because you... didn't... I never said I'd—"

"Oh, heavens, no! I've already made out the check for Ginny's first semester. I'll mail it the minute I get home. You married Rafe, all legal and proper. That was the deal and you fulfilled your end of it."

Air whooshed out of Kate's lungs. Thank God.

"But you told me when you married Enrique that you wanted children, and when my friends started coming up with baby pictures, I expected to have some to show. But then—"

"Aunt Lilith, I'm not having children." *And I'm not your daughter, so you wouldn't be a grandmother, damn it!* "It's too... I'm past thirty and—"

"Nonsense. You have plenty of time and I'll bet Rafe would love some, wouldn't you, Rafe?"

"Well, I—"

"I didn't mean to put you on the spot, dear boy, but I've seen the way you look at Katherine. You're crazy about her, and she'd make a wonderful mother. One of your buddies and his wife are having a baby soon, right?"

"Yes, ma'am."

"This is the perfect place to raise them, on a ranch, wide open spaces. I can tell just by looking at you that you'll make a great father. You two will have beautiful babies. You shouldn't give up that dream, kitten."

"Aunt Lilith?"

"Yes, kitten?"

"Could you please not call me that anymore?"

"Kitten? But I've always—"

"It makes me feel like a child, and I'm not a child."

"Well, of course you're not, but it's an endearment. And it's cute."

"That's the problem. Kittens are cute and little, too young to be on their own."

"What would you like me to call you, then?"

"Kate. Please."

"All right. Kate it is. Listen, shouldn't we go inside and get changed?"

"Yes, I'll be in soon. I just need to talk to Rafe about something."

"Then I'll see you both later." She tucked the rattle back into the box Kate still held. Then she smiled at Rafe. "Talk her into this, okay? I'll bet you can." With a wave of her hand, she turned and walked back to the house.

Kate slapped the lid on the box so hard it wouldn't go on right. "Stupid box! Why isn't it—"

"Here." Rafe gently pried it from her clenched hands, realigned the lid and pushed it down. "Want me to make this go away?"

"*Please*. How could she?"

"You know the answer." He picked up the bag and shoved the box inside. "She's a self-indulgent woman who thinks she can maneuver people into arranging their lives to suit her wishes."

"And she has money to use as leverage!"

"That, too."

He glanced at the turquoise bag. "Maybe Isabel and CJ would like the rattle for Cleo Marie."

She made a face. "I doubt it."

"I doubt it, too. It's not their style. We'll figure out something. But I'll keep it out of sight until we do."

"Thank you." She looked at him. "She was right about one thing. You do want kids and you'd make a great father. That's probably why I'm so angry. She reminded me that what I'm doing is not fair to—"

"Stop right there." He put down the bag and drew her into his arms. "I don't want to hear that ever again."

"But it's true." Interesting position. Until now, he'd only held her for brief moments when they'd been dancing and once two months ago when he'd kissed her until she was breathless. Hugs hadn't been in their repertoire. Self-preservation?

"No, it's not true." He held her firmly without putting any pressure into the embrace. "I'm doing exactly what I want to do, helping you get that money for Ginny."

She looked up at him. "And I appreciate that." This was nothing like dancing. Or even hugging. This was full-body contact when neither of them moved, which was a whole other thing.

An exciting thing. His thigh muscles flexed. Her hands had ended up on his chest, which moved gently in and out as he breathed. The thud of his heart vibrated against her palm. Gradually the beat increased.

He didn't let her go. He didn't back away. "What about tonight?"

She swallowed. "You need to sleep in the cottage."

"There's a fair amount of square footage in the cottage. Could you be more specific?"

"You can have Millie's old room."

"I had a feeling."

"Rafe, I—"

"Millie's room is fine. But I don't have pajamas. And I'm not sleeping in my clothes."

Heat sluiced through her body. Could he tell? "Do you sleepwalk?"

He smiled. "I don't think so. Do you?"

"I don't think so."

"Then this should work out, shouldn't it?"

She nodded, not at all sure. Now her heart was beating as fast as his.

"Nick's on his way over here. I need to get going." Leaning down, he gave her a quick kiss. "See you soon." He grabbed the turquoise bag.

"See you soon." It came out in a whisper, because she didn't have enough breath for anything more.

21

Rafe didn't say anything to Nick until they were in the truck headed back to the bunkhouse. He was still sorting things out, himself. Finally he settled back in the seat and let out a breath. "I'm sure you have questions."

"You got answers?"

"Not many. It's a complicated dance."

"I see that, but from my vantage point, you're in a better position than you were a few hours ago. The way I have it figured, you'll be spending the night in the cottage."

"In Millie's old room."

"Which is right across the hall from—"

"I'm aware. But she doesn't want to have sex."

"That's not what it looked like from the cheap seats, buddy. She was into that post-vows kiss."

"She didn't want to be."

"So what? Just now she didn't seem unhappy to be exchanging body heat with you, either. It's the Brotherhood's considered opinion that you have a shot. And you should take it."

"This sounds too damned familiar, Nicholas. A couple of months ago you recommended I take a shot. Look what happened."

"Yeah, but this is different."

"Is it? Eventually Lilith will go home and life just might return to normal. In the meantime, if Kate and I have a big blowup because I took my shot, as you recommend, we're right back where we were in August. Only worse, because Kate and I might not rebound from a second fight."

"Okay, so you don't think it's worth the risk, but—"

"If it was just me sticking my neck out and I'd be the only one hurt, I'd do it. But it's not just about me. It's about this happy little group we have. What affects one affects us all."

"So you're going to play it safe and stay in your assigned space?"

"That's what she wants."

"Are you sure about that?"

"No, damn it. Which is why I'm taking condoms."

"Good man."

* * *

Rafe had vowed to keep his distance from Lilith during the reception around the fire pit. She was making that difficult. Maybe because she believed he could make her pseudo-grandchildren dreams come true, she dogged him all evening.

She managed to corner him when he was fetching Kate a refill of her champagne. "I'll say one thing for cowboys. They're strong. I've never seen someone balance a case of champagne on his head and carry it up a hill. Actually, I'll say two things. Cowboys are polite, but this *yes, ma'am* stuff makes me feel ancient."

That was his cue to assure her she wasn't ancient. He held his tongue. Henri had told him he didn't have to suck up. But saying nothing was borderline rude and saying *yes, ma'am* would be a smartass response.

Kate must have caught the tail end of Lilith's comment, because she swooped in to rescue him. "I've come to treasure cowboy manners."

"Clearly you've found one who treasures you. I can see my niece is in good hands, Rafe."

"Yes, ma'am." What the heck. It was his automatic response, especially to his elders. She wouldn't want to hear that, either.

"How about *yes, Lilith*? Could you do that for me?"

"I can try, ma'am."

She exhaled. "Well, try harder."

"Yes, ma—"

"Enough." She held up a hand. Then she glanced around. "I'd love to have another one of those cheeseburger sliders. There was a tray going around, but—"

"I'll see if I can locate Jake." He handed Kate her champagne and went in search of his brother, the mastermind behind this delicious finger food.

He found him in conference with Garrett, the other magician in the kitchen. How they'd whipped up such a feast on short notice was beyond him. They had skills.

Jake glanced up. "Nick says you're packing raincoats when you go to the cottage tonight. Excellent decision."

"He told you?"

"Why wouldn't he? We're all invested. We want to make sure you're covering your bases, so to speak."

Rafe muttered something unprintable. Then he took a restorative gulp from his champagne flute. "I came over here because Lilith would like some more of those delicious cheeseburger sliders."

"They're good, aren't they? I got the idea after Millie and I ate some at the drive-in movie."

"They are good, and they're a big hit with Kate's aunt. She's over by the ice chest. I said I'd—"

"Go back and make sure she holds her position. I'll swing by with a tray. Did she mention the mini quiches? Garrett's proud of those."

"She didn't, but I will. Those were spectacular, Garrett. I lost count after three."

"Glad you liked 'em."

Rafe returned to Kate and Lilith. "Jake will be here in—"

"Two shakes of a lamb's tail!" Jake appeared, all smiles, with a tray full of cheeseburger sliders and a few of Garrett's mini quiches.

Lilith blinked. "That was quick."

"Yes, ma'am." Jake gave her a big smile.

She groaned. "I'm in an echo chamber. But I'm crazy about those cheeseburger sliders. Thank you for bringing them." She scooped two on her plate and added a mini quiche. "Many thanks."

Jake favored her with another smile. "Yes, ma'am."

Lilith rolled her eyes. She waited until Jake left before turning to Kate and lowering her voice. "That one... he seems... not quite right."

Rafe laughed. "Jake would love hearing that."

"Oh, don't tell him I said so. I mean, it's charitable of Henrietta to hire someone who isn't all there, but she really shouldn't put him in charge of things like handling valuable luggage."

Kate nodded as if taking the comment seriously. "I'll mention it to her."

"You should. I mean, he didn't damage my bags, but when he saw them, he stroked them and apologized to the alligator who gave its life. Can you imagine?"

Rafe grinned. "I can imagine that very well."

"It's not funny, Rafe. That boy needs help."

"I won't argue the point, but he's a heck of a cook. He and Garrett made all the food for this reception."

"They did? Now that's impressive. I wondered how that was handled, since it wouldn't be appropriate for Kate to do it. Did Jake study with a professional chef?"

Rafe shook his head. "He just has inborn talent. He cooked all the meals at the bunkhouse until recently. He also manages our raptor sanctuary, which is—"

"Raptors? Like velociraptors in that movie?"

"Like eagles, hawks, owls, sometimes a falcon or two."

"Oh, birds. Why do you need a sanctuary for them? Don't they pretty much take care of themselves?"

"They would," Kate said, "except they have to deal with issues caused by humans." Her tone had a slight edge.

"In this country?" Lilith swept her hand in the air. "With all this room? I can't believe there's a problem."

Kate's jaw clenched, a warning sign that she was spoiling for a fight. She might choose this topic because it was handy.

"You know what?" He wrapped an arm around her tense shoulders. "I just noticed that CJ's over there playing his heart out and nobody's dancing. I'll bet they're waiting for us. I'm no expert on this, but I think we're supposed to start it off."

"Why yes, you are." Lilith beamed at him. "But you haven't cut the cake yet, either."

Rafe didn't hesitate. "That'll be after the dance."

"Which isn't how it's usually done, but this is such an unorthodox reception I shouldn't be surprised."

Kate stiffened. "We—"

"Come on, sweetheart." Rafe gripped her more firmly. "Let's go ask CJ for our favorite song. Will you please excuse us, Lilith?"

"Absolutely."

He guided her out of the potential war zone. "It's not worth it," he murmured.

She sighed. "I know, but how *dare* she criticize this wedding? Everybody's worked so hard, and it was lovely, and I..." She sniffed. "Damn, now I'm weepy."

"Want to take a moment?"

She nodded.

He changed course, keeping his arm around her shoulder until they reached the shadows beyond the sparkly lights in the trees and the glow from the fire pit. Then he turned her to face him. "I know it's tough, but if you can rise above it, she won't be here long."

She carefully thumbed the moisture from her eyes so she wouldn't spoil her makeup. "God, I hope not."

"This isn't her kind of place. Soon she'll be winging her way back to Indianapolis and the life she knows. Just focus on the good part. She's written the first check and will mail it this week."

"You're absolutely right." She looked up at him. "Are we really going to dance?"

He smiled. "Seemed like as good an excuse as anything."

"Thanks. I was ready to blow."

"I could tell. And it could be true that everyone's waiting for us."

"Or it could be they're gorging themselves on the terrific meal and saving the dancing for when they're ready to work it off. That's more likely."

"Maybe. But just in case, let's go with the plan."

"We don't have a favorite song."

I do. "How about the one CJ played when you walked up the aisle? It's a waltz and I think that's normally what couples choose for a first dance."

"The Rascal Flatts one?"

"Yeah."

"Did you ask him to play that?"

"No. I had no input on the music. I wondered if you—"

"I didn't, either. I didn't even think about it until the ceremony was about to start. I asked Henri and she said CJ had it under control."

"Did you like what he chose?"

"I did. Very much."

"Me, too. Let's ask him to play *I Won't Let Go.*"

"Okay." She cocked her head and gazed at him. "I just thought of something. Ed took a video of the wedding, and she's been taking more tonight. But Aunt Lilith is here, so we don't need the video, after all."

But he wanted it. No matter what. "Ed's having fun and we might get a laugh out of it someday."

"I suppose."

"Speaking of keeping up appearances, it'll look better if we walk back over there holding hands."

"Better for Lilith?"

"For her, and everybody else, so they know we're not fighting."

"Are people worried about that?"

"Some. Full disclosure, so am I."

She reached for his hand and slipped her fingers through us. "I'm not going to fight with you, Rafe. You're my knight in shining armor."

He exhaled and gave her hand a squeeze. "Yes, ma'am."

22

Until today, Kate hadn't truly held hands with Rafe. Dancing at the Moose required touching hands, and helping her in and out of the truck did, too.

But weaving their fingers together and keeping them locked in place was more intimate. When he'd slid his fingers through hers at the altar, she'd needed that firm grip, that closeness to keep her steady. Now, walking back to the group, she no longer needed it. But she wanted it.

She wanted him. Spending the night in bed with Rafe sounded like a fabulous idea. If she chose to, she could have that experience. But giving in to temptation would be the most selfish thing she'd ever done. It would deepen a relationship that had no future.

CJ was finishing up a George Strait classic when they approached. Nobody was dancing but everybody was listening, as evidenced by the applause and whistles when the tune ended.

"Ol' George would be jealous, bro," Rafe said. "I do believe you do that one better than he does."

"I agree." Kate smiled. "I didn't get a chance to thank you for your contribution to the wedding. You were awesome."

"Glad you liked it." CJ balanced his guitar on his thigh and draped his arm over it. "Time was short and Henri told me to make the selections myself. I tried to pick what I thought you guys might want."

"You did a great job," Rafe said. "In fact, if you wouldn't mind, we'd like a repeat of *I Won't Let Go* for our first dance."

"Ah, yes, the first dance! I wondered if we were doing that."

"Rafe thought of it just now. Is that why nobody's started? They're waiting for us?"

CJ laughed. "In a way. A few people have asked me, and I didn't know if you wanted to go that route or not. I was about ready to find you and ask. I mean, you don't *have* to do it if you—"

"I'd like to." Rafe glanced at her. "And I think Kate's okay with it."

"I am."

"You guys do a good job with a waltz and it's a nice tune. It won't be so easy to glide around on dead grass, but I'm sure you're up to the challenge."

Rafe squeezed her hand. "We are."

CJ sat up straighter and wrapped his fingers around the neck of the guitar. Then he paused. "One other thing. Traditionally, after the bride and groom dance, the bride dances with her father and the groom dances with his mother."

"Let's not get into that," Kate said. "Rafe has Henri, but I don't have anyone, so it makes no sense to go there."

Rafe nodded. "Agreed."

"Then after you're done I'll just invite everyone out to dance. Let me get their attention." He raised his voice. "Hey, folks. Gather round for Kate and Rafe's first dance as a married couple."

A married couple. Nobody had used that phrase until now. But it was the accepted language for this part of the evening and CJ, like everyone here, was out to fool Aunt Lilith. He played the opening for *I Won't Let* Go.

Rafe held out his hand and she moved into his strong arms. She'd loved waltzing with him from the first time he'd invited her to dance at the Moose.

He took charge tonight the way he had then—his gaze warm and steady, his big hand pressed firmly to the middle of her back, his smile coaxing an answering one from her. Had the waltz been the beginning? Had he been wooing her from the start?

Now that she was in his arms, surrounded by the people who'd become her dearest friends, she accepted what her heart had known all along. She'd fallen for the Buckskin gang the first night they'd taken her to the Choosy Moose. And she'd fallen for Rafe Banner that same night when he'd asked her to waltz.

Had they danced to this very song? Possibly. The lyrics were pure Rafe—a promise of never-ending support, no matter what life dished out. He'd provide firm ground under her feet when the world began to shake and a buffer when the wind threatened to blow her over.

The song ended and he pulled her close, kissed her softly, and smiled. "Thank you."

"My pleasure." As everyone around her cheered, she held the moment close. Soon enough she'd have to make some tough choices, live through some trying times. But for now, she was filled with gratitude for her blessings.

Rafe gave her hand a squeeze. "Let's go cut that fancy cake."

She laughed. "Follow my lead. I'm a professional."

* * *

Kate was in no rush to leave the party. Rafe seemed just as willing to drag things out. But Isabel wasn't a late-night partier now that she was almost seven months along. When she and CJ left, the live music went with them. Leo hooked up the speakers for his phone, but it wasn't the same.

Matt and Lucy said their goodbyes not long after that. When Ben and Henri were ready to go, Ben offered to take Lilith, too.

"Oh, I'll just ride back with Kate and Rafe," she said with a wave of her hand. "You'll take me, won't you, kids?"

"Yes, ma'am." Rafe shot a quick look at Kate. "Be glad to."

Henri glanced at Kate and rolled her eyes. "Ben, will you excuse me a minute? I need to have a quick word with Kate."

"Sure thing."

Henri took her arm and pulled her far enough away that Aunt Lilith wouldn't be able to hear. "I sense that she's going to make a nuisance of herself."

"That's what she does best."

"The less time you and Rafe spend with her, the better. I don't want this thing falling apart."

"What can she do? We got married."

"She's only paid part of the tuition, right?"

"Yes, but I think she's good for the rest of it."

"Just to be on the safe side, I'm taking charge of her tomorrow. I'll keep her occupied so you and Rafe can work this out however you choose without worrying about her snooping into your business."

"Henri, that's asking too much. I—"

"It's what your mother would do if she were here. Let me help."

"But—"

"I want to, sweetheart. For you and for Rafe."

"All right. After this is over, I'll—"

"After this is over we'll have another party, a real one." She gave Kate a quick hug. "Besides, you and Rafe are doing me a favor. If she's not going home with Ben and me, that gives us a little time to enjoy being alone in the house."

"Okay." Kate laughed. "Now I feel better."

After Henri and Ben left, the number of guests dwindled rapidly. Garrett and Jake started cleaning up and everyone who was still there helped, including Kate and Rafe.

Millie drew Kate aside as she was tying up a garbage bag. "This is silly. You shouldn't be cleaning up after your own wedding reception."

"But—"

"I know why you're procrastinating, but you have to face the music sometime. Put on your big-girl panties. Or take them off. Either way, I hope you know we all love you and that big lug, no matter what."

She sighed. "You're right. I'll get my jacket and Aunt Lilith's."

"Attagirl. By the way, you have my permission to just swing by the big house and shove her out."

Kate grinned. "Kinda hard to do from the front seat."

"You know what I mean. Not literally. But don't let Rafe walk her to the damn door. That woman has some solid brass ones, inviting herself to ride home with you guys."

"As Rafe says, we have to rise above it. She'll be gone soon."

"Not soon enough for me." Millie hesitated. "Did you have a little bit of fun today? Despite the circumstances?"

"I did. I'm going to write thank you notes to every single person who put themselves out to make this happen, especially you and Henri."

"We just want you to be happy."

"I am. Aunt Lilith's mailing the first check next week."

"I wish she'd just give Ginny the full amount. Partial payments make me nervous."

"Aunt Lilith will keep the money flowing if I keep sending her chirpy updates she can share with her friends."

"I hope you're right." She lowered her voice. "Rumor has it Rafe's sleeping in my old room tonight."

"That rumor is correct. We're not having sex."

Millie smiled as if she didn't believe a word of it and gave her a hug. "Jake and I are outta here."

"We'll be right behind you." After Millie and Jake said their goodbyes, Kate gave Rafe and her aunt the word that she'd like to go home.

Emotion flickered in Rafe's eyes. "I'll get my duffle."

"Your duffle?" Aunt Lilith's eyebrows rose. "You don't have your things down at Kate's cottage already?"

He winced. "Um, sure. I just need to take the rental outfit down there so we can return it on Monday. No reason to leave it at the bunkhouse."

"You're shoving it into a duffle? Didn't the rental place provide you with a garment bag?"

"Um, yes, but I—"

"Oh, my God, I get it! You haven't been living with Kate, have you?"

"Well, not exactly, but we... I'll be right back with my duffle." He left, his long strides taking him quickly toward the bunkhouse.

Aunt Lilith pinned Kate with a stare. "Have you slept with him?"

"I don't think that's any of your—"

"That's answer enough. You haven't. I'm so *impressed* with that, kit--Kate. I assumed when you came up with a husband so fast, you'd been sleeping with someone and this was the nudge that you needed to finally make that commitment."

"Rafe's a bit old-fashioned." True, right?

"I *love* that. He clearly adores you, yet he wouldn't take that step until after you were married. How exciting. He's one in a million. Aren't you glad I gave you this push?"

No. "I'm sure it will work out well for everyone." Not as sure as she'd been about those root beer floats, though.

"Ready to go, ladies?" Rafe appeared, duffle in hand, his sheepskin coat on and his hat pulled low. Hiding.

She wouldn't mind having a Stetson to pull over her eyes. "Let's go."

Rafe opened both front and back doors of his truck and asked Aunt Lilith to please wait while he handed Kate into the passenger seat. She waited, clearly dazzled.

After Rafe started the truck and pulled out, she leaned forward and put a hand on each of their shoulders. "I'm going to give you kids a honeymoon. Where would you like to go? Tahiti? Paris? Singapore?"

Rafe sent Kate a wide-eyed look.

She wasn't fazed by the offer. This was classic Aunt Lilith behavior. She withheld approval and material rewards until she got her way, and then she gave extravagantly to those she'd bent to her will.

Turning toward her aunt, she managed a smile. "That's incredibly generous of you, but we'd need a couple of weeks to truly enjoy any of those places, and we can't be gone that long. Henri couldn't spare either of us."

"Nonsense. Jake could do your job and—"

"He's managing the raptor sanctuary."

"That can't take much time. If Henri can throw together a wedding at a moment's notice, she can figure out how to give you and Rafe two weeks for a honeymoon. I'll talk to her in the morning."

"Please don't. I can't speak for Rafe, but I want to start our new life right here at the Buckskin."

He nodded. "That suits me, too, Lilith. I appreciate the offer, but Kate and I don't need anything but each other. I'd rather have you put that money towards Ginny's schooling."

"Oh, my God, you're such a heroic man, Rafe. There must be something I can do for the two of you."

How about leaving on the next available flight? "We really don't need anything, Aunt Lilith, but if you're determined to give us something, a donation to Raptors Rise in our name would be fantastic. We'd be eternally grateful, wouldn't we, Rafe?"

"Yes, ma'am." His voice sounded funny, like he was choking back laughter. "I can't think of a wedding present I'd treasure more than that."

"Consider it done. But I'll come up with something else, too, something more interesting and personal. I can always ship it after I get home."

Rafe pulled up in front of Henri's house, shut off the engine and opened his door. "Hang tight, ma'am. I'll walk you in."

Of course he would. His training went too deep to let her walk to the door alone. On top of that, she was donating to Raptors Rise. Kate settled back in her seat and waited for his return.

He opened the door and climbed in. "Fast thinking on the sanctuary donation. Jake will be excited."

"You wouldn't rather go to Paris?"

He started the engine. "I'd go anywhere if it was with you."

Her breath caught. "Rafe, I—"

"I'm in love with you." He swung the truck around and drove back down the hill. "Simple as that. And because I'm in love with you, I'm going to sleep in Millie's old room because you want me to."

"I do." Mostly when her better self was in charge.

"I didn't put a change of clothes in that duffle. Couldn't see the point since I couldn't picture myself shaving and showering in your bathroom. I'll do that in the bunkhouse in the morning."

"Oh." She glanced over her shoulder at the duffle sitting on the backseat. "Then why did you bring it?"

"I have my toothbrush in there."

"You could have stuck that in your pocket."

"I also brought my insurance policy."

"Your *insurance policy*? You want me to look it over in case you die in the middle of the night? What the hell, Rafe?"

His chuckle had an intimate, sexy undertone. "It's not paperwork." He pulled in front of the cottage, cut the engine and turned to her. His left hand rested on the wheel and his ring caught the light. "It's a box of condoms. In case you change your mind."

23

The interior of Rafe's cab was dim, but there was no mistaking the gleam of excitement in Kate's eyes. Or the sharp intake of breath. Gave him a smidgen of hope.

"I won't change my mind." Her voice quivered. "I can't."

"Why not?"

"Because I don't want to be married. The minute I signed the marriage license today I felt the bars closing in on me. I'm in a contractual agreement that I can't break until Ginny's out of school. I'm trapped. It's for a good cause, but that doesn't mean I feel good about it."

"On Monday we'll check out the post-nup. Will that help?"

"Probably. But do you see what I mean? Why I can't sleep with you?"

"I'm not talking about sleeping."

"Oh, for heaven's sake, I know what you're talking about. Sex."

"Making love."

"Same thing."

"If you believe that, then you really need to get educated on the subject. And I'm just the guy to teach you."

"You don't see what a mistake that would be?"

"No, I don't. Enrique cheated on you and he left you with mountains of debt when he ran off to Mexico with his girlfriend. It goes without saying he didn't love you. He never loved you."

"So he never loved me. So what?"

"Have you ever had sex with a man who loved you?"

"Probably not, and thank you kindly for pointing that out. Now I feel like a pathetic loser."

"That makes two of us."

She hesitated. "What do you mean?"

"I started falling for you on day one. It's been building for more than two years. When I compare how I feel about you to what I felt for the women I've had sex with, women I *thought* I loved… no comparison."

She took a shaky breath. "And I'm all wrong for you. I'm so sorry."

"About what? It's not your fault that I'm in this deep. You've warned me and everyone on this ranch that you'd never marry again."

"And going to bed with you will only make things worse."

"It can't get any worse. I have a chance to find out what it's like to make love with a woman I really love. You're denying me that chance. What's worse than that?"

"I don't know."

"I don't, either." He opened his door. "I'll get you down." He took the time to grab the duffle out of the backseat. She might not wait for him to let her out.

But she did. She put her hand in his although she didn't meet his gaze. "Look, it's late and we're both tired." She stepped to the ground and let go of his hand.

"Speak for yourself. I'm wide awake."

"That's adrenaline." She started toward the porch steps.

That's love. "Are you saying we should sleep on it?"

"I'm saying I want you to stay in Millie's room."

"That was my plan. Mind if I borrow your toothpaste?"

She glanced at him, gave him a small smile. "I don't mind. You can have the bathroom first."

"Eager to get me tucked away for the night?"

"Yes, I am." She climbed the steps.

"Out of sight, out of mind?"

"I can only hope."

"Oh, you're capable of a lot more than hope." He crossed the porch so he could hold the screen door for her.

She went inside the darkened cottage. "See you in the morning."

He came in behind her. "Technically, that begins one minute after midnight." He closed and locked the door.

"Not in this house." She walked straight through the living room to the hall. "Goodnight,

Rafe." She went into her bedroom and closed the door with a soft click.

He'd prepared for this scenario. He wasn't thrilled with her response to his argument, but at least he'd made it.

After her speech about feeling trapped, he had to face the truth. She had a phobia. And she might never get over it.

* * *

Millie's room used to have a king bed in it, one she'd bought for herself. Rafe had helped move it to the cabin Jake and Millie built in the woods near the raptor sanctuary. So now the old double bed was back where the king had been.

After sleeping in a bunk that was too small for more than ten years, Rafe was used to accommodating himself to whatever sleeping conditions he'd been given. The double bed would afford him more room than his bunk since he could lie on the diagonal.

The bedside table held a decent-sized lamp. A smaller one with a nightlight bulb sat on top of the dresser. He left that on and turned off the big lamp. If Kate came into the room, and that was doubtful, he wanted some illumination.

Lying crossways on the bed meant the sheets and blankets were somewhat jacked, but he worked with them and managed to achieve coverage. The house was cool and he was naked, so coverage was a good thing.

Well, not completely naked. He wore a ring, something he wasn't accustomed to. Strange sensation, having that metal band around his third finger. He could take it off, but then he might lose it.

He stretched out in the semi-darkness, heart pounding, and listened. Water ran in the bathroom. Bare feet whispered up and down the hall. He held his breath.

She didn't pause beside his open door, let alone step through it. Her door closed with a crisp snap of hardware. Again. He prided himself on his mental toughness. She was tougher.

A wise man would get some rest, gather his strength for tomorrow. He stared into the darkness and willed her to come to him. Didn't work worth a damn.

Aunt Lilith was a pain in the ass and he wished she'd leave, but maybe not quite yet. When she was in residence, he had to sleep in the cottage, sleep being a relative term.

It could mean actual sleep, or it could mean lying awake longing for Kate's soft body. Or it could mean rolling around on this bed and making love until dawn. If given the chance, he'd choose Option C.

Gradually the adrenaline pumping through his system found other things to do and he drifted into a grayish world of semi-reality. When a woman appeared in the open doorway, her curvy body clad in a filmy nightgown backlit by a baseboard light in the hall, he doubted his senses.

He struggled toward full consciousness as the product of his imagination approached the bed.

"That's a weird way to lie in bed."

Sounded like Kate's voice, but she was supposed to walk into his room saying things like

I'm going crazy over there! or *Take me, Rafe! Take me now!*

A critique of his sleeping position hadn't been part of the fantasy. He fought off the urge to slide back into oblivion and sat up. "Kate?"

"I couldn't sleep, but clearly you've had no problem."

"I wasn't asleep."

"The hell you weren't. You had a little snore going on."

"Was it bad?"

"Not so bad." She moved closer to the bed. "While you were snoring, I was thinking."

"Oh?" *Don't get your hopes up, dude.*

"You're right that I've never had sex with a man who loved me. Have you ever had sex with a woman who loved you?"

Even half-asleep, he had that answer. "No."

"So you need this as much as I do."

"I'm not totally awake yet, but did you just say you love me?"

"In a round-about way, yes, I did."

That cleared the cobwebs from his brain right quick. "You love me?"

"Of course. Didn't you—"

"Absolutely not! I dreamed and I hoped, but I didn't *know*. How could I? You turned me down flat in August."

"Well, I do, and you should have sex with a woman who loves you. Don't you think?"

"Kate, what's happening here? I love you and you love me. We just got married. Why aren't we doing it like bunnies and shouting hallelujah?"

"Because I don't want to be married to you, or anybody. And if we have sex, which I'm seriously considering—"

"Thank God."

"I don't want you to think that means I want to live with you. I never want to go through that again."

"Go through what?"

"Cheating was the final straw, and leaving me in debt was awful, but our daily life was awful, too. Everything had to be his way."

"You didn't see that coming?"

"How could I? He courted me, took me to dinner, promised me the moon. But once he put a ring on my finger—" She held up her left hand. The ring was still there. "Everything changed."

"So if I promise not to be a jerk, you won't believe me."

"No."

"So why are you here?"

"Because we love each other. We even *like* each other. And maybe… maybe we should get the chance to feel what it's like to have that kind of sex, since Aunt Lilith's forcing us to be in the same house."

His blood pumped faster and most of it was headed to a predictable destination. "And when she leaves?"

"We quit while we're ahead."

He groaned. "Kate…"

"Okay, you're right. It's a terrible idea. I don't know what I was thinking." She turned and started for the door.

He was out of bed, his hand gripping her arm before she'd taken two steps. "Don't go."

"I have to. That groan was pitiful. You—"

"I'll do it." He drew her close, dizzy with wanting her. "I'll take that deal."

24

Caught in Rafe's strong arms and pressed against his aroused body, Kate's resistance crumbled. "Then kiss me. Make me forget this is a huge mistake."

"You bet." His hungry mouth sought hers.

With a whimper, she wrapped her arms around his broad back and hung on as he kissed her as thoroughly as he had in a forested glen two months ago. She'd ached for him then. And denied herself.

But now... as he plunged his tongue into her mouth, as he cupped her bottom in his big hands and fit his hips to hers, she craved him more than air.

Panting, she wiggled free and wrenched off her nightgown. "Get the—"

"Yes, ma'am." He crossed the room and unzipped the duffle.

She tossed her nightgown on the floor. "You didn't put them in the bedside table drawer?"

"Seemed like tempting fate." He ripped open a packet.

She glanced at him—tall, muscular, big all over. As he rolled a condom over that bad boy, the clench of desire made her gasp. "You sure are tempting me." She eyed the bed. "Too damned small." She threw back the covers. "But mine's no better."

"It's what we've got." He was beside her in two strides and swept her up in his arms. "We'll do it crossways." He laid her down gently, her head on the far pillow and her feet on the opposite corner.

His gaze swept over her and he swallowed. She held out her arms. "Come here, you."

"Just lookin'." His chest heaved. "You're... I knew you'd be beautiful. That's if I ever had the chance to..." His gaze met hers. "This better not be a dream."

"If it is, you'd better get to it before you wake up."

"Good point." He moved over her, nudged her thighs farther apart and braced his weight on his forearms. "I still can't believe you came to me."

She quivered in anticipation as she slid her palms up his furred chest. "I've wanted you for a long time, too. I've fantasized what you'd look like naked."

"I've fantasized you naked, too." His gaze drifted to her breasts. "The reality is better."

"Way better. You're like one of those Greek statues, but more generously endowed."

He smiled. "That's why I'm gonna take it slow."

"I can handle you, Rafe Banner."

"I have no doubt." He leaned down and feathered a kiss over her mouth as he settled into position. "But there's no reason to hurry."

"That's what you think. I'm liable to start this party without you if you don't... oh, my." She gulped as he eased slowly into her entrance. Closing her eyes, she savored the heat, the warmth, the snug fit. "That's... a lot."

"I love you, Kate."

The low timbre of his voice sent a message straight to her core. She opened her eyes.

"I love you." He sank deeper.

The intensity in his dark eyes stunned her into silence. Wrapping him in her arms, heart beating wildly, she surrendered. His thick cock claimed more territory, then more.

The light in his eyes burned brighter. "I love everything about you—your voice, your laugh." Leaning down, he kissed her again. "Even your stubbornness."

"I'm stub—"

"But not too stubborn to cross the hall." He eased in another fraction, kissed her again.

She closed her eyes, awash in emotions stirred by the tenderness in his voice, the gradual, gentle blending of his body with hers.

"I love that you beat me at poker. I love the way you dance." He pushed once more and he was there, in full possession of her most intimate space.

She dug her fingers into his muscled back as the solid length of him set off mini-explosions. She gulped. "Some... of me is... dancing... now."

"I know. I can feel it. I love you, Kate." And he began to move.

She sucked in a breath. "Holy Macarena."

He smiled and kept going.

And she lost her mind. Crying out his name. she arched beneath him as waves of splendor crashed over her again and again. Best. Climax. Ever.

He buried his cock deep and absorbed the shock waves. As they faded, he dragged in a breath. With a soft murmur of *again*, he began to stroke, increasing the pace.

Helpless in the clutch of sensual pleasure, she hurtled toward the abyss a second time, panting and slick with sweat. Surging forward, he set off the explosion.

She cried out and he echoed her cries. Gasping her name, his big body shook and shivered in the grip of his climax. She rode it out with him, holding on tight as he shuddered in her arms.

Gently she stroked his back, her body sated, her heart full. "I love you."

Lifting his head, he met her gaze. "Tell me again."

"I love you, Rafe."

His chest heaved and he closed his eyes. When he opened them, they sparkled with happiness. "If I *should* die in the middle of the night—"

"Which you won't! Good grief."

"I know, but if I did, I'd be okay with that."

"Well, I wouldn't!"

"Are you saying you'd like me to stick around a little longer?"

"I want you to stick around for a very long time. It's just that we—" She stopped herself. Now wasn't the time. "Would you... would you like some cocoa?"

He laughed. "Sure, why not?"

"I don't know why I want cocoa, but—"

"I do. Last December we had that big snowfall."

"And we built forts and had snowball fights. Followed by cocoa. And you almost kissed me under the mistletoe."

"And chickened out."

She stroked his cheek. "This makes up for it."

"Oh, I wouldn't say that." He grinned. "I think I need to make it up to you some more."

"After cocoa."

"Yeah, after cocoa." He eased away from her. "Meet you in the kitchen." He left the bed and headed for the bathroom.

"FYI, I'm fetching my bathrobe," she called after him.

"Then I'll put on my jeans," he called back.

She climbed out of bed, picked up her nightgown and hurried to her room to get her robe. She put it on as she walked to the kitchen. Flipping on the kitchen light, she washed her hands at the sink before starting the cocoa.

Cocoa powder, sugar, a few teaspoons of water. She made cocoa the way her mom did. No instant for her. She was stirring the mixture into a dark syrup over low heat when Rafe came in dressed in his jeans. He'd put on his shirt, too, but left it unbuttoned.

"Somehow I knew you'd add the shirt."

"Feels slightly more decent since we'll be sitting in the kitchen. I don't think I've ever seen that bathrobe."

"Why would you? You're never here when I'm wearing it."

"Which seems strange, because I feel as if I know you so well, but—"

"Now you know me better."

He grinned. "Yes, ma'am. But why the bathrobe and not the nightgown?"

"I might as well be naked in that nightgown and working naked in the kitchen is weird."

"I guess the nightgown is sort of see-through. I didn't get a good look at it, but it's like something Beth would have in her shop."

"That's where I bought it."

"Not to be nosy, but when?"

She smiled. "None of your business."

"Did you buy it recently?" He walked up behind her and slid his arms around her waist.

"I'm not telling."

He dipped his head and nibbled on her earlobe. "I have ways of making you talk."

Her breath hitched as warmth sluiced through her body. "Do you want cocoa?"

"I thought I did." He untied her robe as he nuzzled the side of her neck. "Do you want cocoa?"

When he slipped his hand inside her robe and cradled her breast, she let the spoon fall against the side of the pan with a clatter. "Maybe... later."

Reaching around her, he switched off the burner. "I'm taking you back to bed." Scooping her up, he carried her out of the kitchen and down the hall.

She wound her arms around his neck. "I love it when you carry me."

"Always dreamed of doing it."

"So have I."

He glanced down at her and smiled. "I'm pretty heavy."

"Smart aleck."

"Did you buy that nightgown for me?"

"You had your insurance policy. I had mine."

"But when?" He walked into the dim bedroom. "You had no time."

"Beth opens at nine. I didn't have to be at Henri's until ten."

He sat her on the edge of the bed. "Where is it?"

"I took it back to my room."

"Where?"

"On my bed. But why—"

"If you bought it for me, I want to see it on you. In better light." He gave her a quick kiss. "Be right back."

"Want me to rummage around in your duffle while you're gone?"

"Absolutely."

She walked over to the duffle, pulled out the box inside and carried it over to the bedside table. Opening the drawer, she dumped the contents, took one out and laid it beside the lamp.

He came in while she still had the drawer open. "Giving them a new home?"

"A more convenient home." She glanced at the nightgown in his hand. "I see you found it."

"Will you wear it for me?"

"I can." She held out her hand. "But the idea is for me to make an entrance. If I just take off my robe and put on the nightgown, it loses something."

He looked amused. "Want to go out and come back in?"

"Yes."

"Okay if I turn on the bedside lamp?"

"Sure." She gave him a once-over. "You're not the only one who wants better light." She stepped out into the darkened hall, slipped off the robe and left it on the floor while she popped the nightgown over her head.

It slithered over her hot skin, making her nipples tighten with anticipation. The nearly transparent material's silver sheen echoed the silver threads in her wedding dress.

The similarity ended there. The nightgown's plunging neckline and short shirt left little to the imagination. She'd driven to town and bought it after her conversation with Rafe on her front porch this morning.

He'd left her in a state of agitation, his words ringing in her ears. *I want you.* Powerful stuff. She hadn't trusted herself to be strong enough to refuse him if he pressed his case again. And if she caved, she'd wanted to look good doing it.

His argument in the truck might have won her over immediately if he hadn't rested his left hand on the steering wheel. But when she'd said no, he'd accepted her decision, leaving her alone to think.

And ache. And eventually cave. Was she sorry? God help her, she was not. Clearly, neither was he.

Were they headed for a cliff? Quite possibly. But they weren't there yet. Picking up her robe, she walked into the light.

25

Rafe almost swallowed his tongue. Kate strolled into the room trailing her robe behind her like a fur coat she'd just shrugged off. The barely-there negligee nearly brought him to his knees.

Her smoky gaze promised unlimited sexual delights. The negligee showcased her toned, supple body. The curve of her breasts peaked out of the scalloped neckline and her taut nipples created a tempting dent in the silvery fabric.

His mouth watered and his cock stood at attention.

The material shimmered as she walked and the hemline teased him with glimpses of her creamy thighs. She dropped the robe, ran her palms over her hips and took a long, slow breath that lifted her breasts and made them quiver.

She gave him a sultry smile. "What do you think?"

"I can't—" He cleared his throat. "I can't think at all."

"Good." She grinned in triumph. "That's what I was going for. Take off your shirt and jeans, please. It's my turn to love you."

"Don't have to ask me twice." He fumbled with the button and zipper.

"I wasn't planning on it, but you look like you need some help."

"I've got it." He wrenched the zipper down and shoved off jeans and briefs in one motion, kicking them aside. He stepped toward the bedside table. "We'll need—"

"I'll take care of that." She shooed him toward the bed. "You don't have to do anything but moan."

He had a hunch he'd be doing a lot of that. He stretched out on his back, his heart playing the bongos, his good soldier standing at attention.

Putting a condom packet between her teeth, Kate crawled onto the bed like a lioness on the prowl. Her position allowed him a spectacular view of her full breasts.

Rejoice in her free will. The phrase from his wedding vows fit this amazing moment. Kate had let her playful vixen loose to taunt and arouse him. He was rejoicing like hell.

Straddling his thighs, she laid the condom aside and wrapped both hands around his pride and joy.

The visual of Kate holding tight to his cock, her wedding ring catching the light, would stay with him for a very long time. "Be careful. It's loaded."

"I can see that. And me with an itchy trigger finger." She squeezed gently.

He gasped.

"Just testing." She ran her knuckle up and down the underside.

He moaned.

"Very good." She held his length in both hands again. "You're lovely."

"Thanks." The area on his thighs where she'd parked her sweet self was growing warm. And damp. He bracketed her hips. "Gonna use that raincoat anytime soon?"

"Of course, silly." She stroked him lightly with her fingernail.

He moaned again and clenched his jaw. "How soon?"

"When would you like?"

"Now would be good." His voice was getting scratchy.

"First I need to ditch this." Crossing her arms, she reached for the hem of her nightgown and pulled it slowly over her head, gradually giving him what he'd craved, her luscious body bathed in lamplight.

"Glorious."

She smiled. "Glad you like it."

"I love it." Sliding his hands up her sides, he cupped her breasts and brushed his thumbs over her nipples.

She shivered. "That's very nice, but if you keep doing it, I'll probably never get the condom on."

"You drive a hard bargain." He released her and lowered his arms.

"I do want to get it on." She opened the packet and had him sheathed in no time. "I'm getting a little antsy, myself."

"Music to my ears." Good thing she'd made short work of the process. He was losing ground in the battle for control of his climax.

Rising to her knees, she made the initial connection, flattened her palms against his chest and began the slow process of taking him in.

He wasn't going to make it. The added light on her beautiful body, her enraptured expression and the unbelievable friction would bring him down. He'd come early and ruin this precious moment.

Then she spoke. "I love you, Rafe."

Her words pulled him back from the brink. He really, really wanted to hear this. Needed to hear this. He held her gaze.

"I love your loyalty, your generosity and your strength." She eased a little lower. "Not just physical. Mental strength."

Boy, did he need that right now. He clenched his fists and hung on.

"I love you for swallowing your pride and marrying me." She took him deep inside her body and leaned forward, breathless and intense. "I love you, Rafe."

He basked in the glow in her eyes. Yeah, he could die happy, now. He didn't want to, though. There was hope.

Her core muscles contracted. "I can't hold back. I'm—"

"Go with it." As she began to shake, he thrust upward. She gasped and cried out as her climax rolled through her, rolled over his cock and destroyed any chance of holding back.

He erupted with a force that pushed the air from his lungs in a deep, satisfied groan of release. Breathing hard, he closed his eyes in gratitude. If this was all he'd ever have...

No, damn it. He'd fight for her. He'd fight for more. She loved him. That was all he needed to know.

When he opened his eyes, she was staring down at him, her expression earnest. "Was it okay?"

He started laughing.

She frowned. "What's so funny? And by the way, this feels strange, to be connected like this when you're laughing."

He cleared his throat and cupped her face in both hands. "Was it okay? You couldn't tell?"

"Well, you did groan pretty loud, but that might have been disappointment because I came so fast and that made you come fast, too. You might have wanted it to last long—"

"Kate, every second I'm naked with you I'm happier than I've ever been in my entire life."

"Really?"

He held her gaze. "Really. And you're so darned sexy, especially with that nightgown and taking charge like you did, that I was sure I'd come early and disappoint *you.*"

"I can't imagine you losing control. You're a rock. You never—"

"I was losing it from the moment you walked in wearing that nightgown." He brushed his thumbs over her cheekbones. "I'm putty in your hands. Which you just proved. We've made love twice, and each time I thought the top of my head was coming off. It's never been this good. Not for me. I can't speak for you."

"Same here. You were right. Making love with someone you love, who loves you back, is the best."

He longed to press the point, to suggest that two people in that situation would have a different trajectory. Marriage wouldn't become a prison.

But she might put up an argument and he didn't want to argue. "How about that cocoa?"

"You still want it?"

"Yes, ma'am, and brownies if you have any left."

"I do."

"Ready to try switching to the kitchen venue again?"

She smiled. "It's worth a try."

Ten minutes later, after his cleanup routine, he joined her in the kitchen. She had on her robe again, likely with nothing underneath. He resisted the urge to go over and kiss her.

Instead he made for the container of brownies. "Looks like quite a few brownies."

"I always have some on hand."

"You do? I seem to remember you routinely ran out."

"That was when Millie lived here and we'd have you guys over all the time. You'd clean me out. That doesn't happen anymore, especially since..."

"Our fight in August."

"Not just that. The bachelor auction had an impact on more people than us. Nick, the bottomless pit, moved to town to be with Eva."

"So he did. That cowboy could eat his weight in brownies, no problem." He popped the top off the container. "But it was mostly our issue that changed the dynamic. The Buckskin gang can add people, but it's lousy at subtracting them."

"I subtracted myself."

"I know you did. Please don't do that again, especially if it has to do with me. Maybe I've been here longer, but that doesn't mean I get to stay in the group and you have to leave." He turned around, the container in his hand.

"I think it does." She had her back to him as she picked up the saucepan and poured two steaming mugs of cocoa before putting down the pan. "Whipped cream or marshmallows?"

"You don't remember how I like it?"

She glanced at him over her shoulder. "I do, but I'm pretending I don't so you won't think I've been fixated on you."

"I think you have been." He put down the brownie container and gave up the struggle. He had to hold her. "I think we've been fixated on each other for two years." Taking her by the shoulders, he turned her to face him. "I remember you like those baby marshmallows, God knows why. They're disgusting little buggers, especially when they start to melt."

"And you want whipped cream."

"Yes, ma'am." He rubbed his hands up and down her arms. "And you. I want you."

She gazed at him. "I'll always be your friend."

"Is that how you love me, as a friend?"

"Yes."

"That's it?"

"No."

He gripped her arms. "I'm your lover, Kate." *And your husband.* He'd be better off not mentioning that. "We're lovers, now. There's no getting around it. Not after tonight."

26

Kate couldn't argue the point, especially after Rafe made love to her twice more before they finally drifted off to sleep, curled up and cozy in the double bed.

She woke in the gray light of predawn, alone in the bed. The scent of coffee drifted into the room, but the house was still dark. Had he made coffee without turning on a light in the kitchen?

The light over the stove would have helped, but not much. He should have flipped on the overhead. Maybe he was trying to demonstrate he wasn't the kind of man who would change everything to suit him now that she wore his ring.

Her ex never would have made coffee in the dark so he wouldn't disturb her. But he also wouldn't have been up at five in the morning making coffee in any case. The thought of serving anyone breakfast had horrified him, so his restaurant hadn't opened until eleven-thirty.

Kate slipped out of bed, located her robe lying over the back of a rocker in the corner, and put it on as she went out to investigate Rafe's decision to leave off the lights.

She was halfway to the kitchen when he called to her from the living room couch. "I'm here."

She turned. "Sitting in the dark?"

"Couldn't sleep. Didn't want to disturb you. Did the coffee wake you up?"

"I don't know what woke me, but it wasn't the coffee." He was dressed, including his boots. His hat lay on the coffee table. He stood as she walked in. "Oh, goodness, please don't get up."

He chuckled. "Telling me not to get up when a woman walks in the room is like asking me to stop breathing."

"But I'm your..." Wow, she'd almost said it.

"All the more reason." He put his mug down. "Want some coffee? I made plenty."

"Yes, please."

"Have a seat. I'll get it."

She settled onto the couch on the middle cushion she usually took. The one on her left was dented. He'd left her spot open.

"You're welcome to turn on a light if you want," he called from the kitchen.

"It's nice like this. Peaceful."

"That's what I thought. I almost went out to the porch, but I would've had to put on my coat." He brought in her coffee. "Can I get a kiss? I promise I'm not trying to start anything."

"Oh?"

"Not that I wouldn't like to, but my beard could scratch you. Besides, I'll be heading down to the bunkhouse soon."

"Okay." Putting her mug on the table, she lifted her face to his. He leaned down and kissed her with gentle restraint.

He raised his head and smiled. "Good morning."

"Same to you."

He resumed his seat and picked up his mug.

She took a sip from hers. "Good coffee, especially if you made it in the dark. You could have turned on a light. I wouldn't have minded."

"It wasn't that tough. Your kitchen's bigger than the one at the bunkhouse and light comes in from the porch. I'm not as likely to whack my head on a cupboard." He glanced at her. "How did it feel, waking up with a man in the house?"

"Déjà vu."

"PTSD?"

"No, fortunately. Enrique wasn't a morning person. He was never up before me. I don't associate him with this time of day."

"Bonus."

"How did it feel waking up in the house with me?"

"Special." His chest heaved. "I felt like leaving the door locked and spending the rest of the day in bed with you."

"Instead of going to the bunkhouse?"

"Yes, ma'am." He swallowed more coffee.

Exciting concept. Delicious, in fact. "I guess we could. I can wash and dry your clothes so you have something clean to wear whenever you decide to get dressed. I have enough food."

"Ahh, I want to." He leaned back against the couch. "But that would be like taking out a billboard ad announcing what went on last night."

"Do you care?"

"More than I thought I would. I mean, this is the Buckskin. Everyone will have it figured out soon enough, no matter what we do. But..." He put down his coffee and turned to her. "Right now, this... whatever it is... belongs to us. I'm not ready to share it with anyone. Not until we have to."

He wanted to guard their privacy. That touched her. Setting her mug on the table, she cupped his bristly face in both hands. "Then we won't share it." She leaned toward him. "Let's seal it with a kiss."

"My beard—"

"I don't care. I want a real kiss."

"Then you'll get one." He cupped the back of her head and took charge. Ah, that was more like it. As the kiss heated up, her robe came undone. Eventually she ended up on his lap with his hand on her breast and his tongue deep in her mouth.

With a groan of frustration, he backed off and tugged her robe closed. "Gotta stop or I'll sabotage the plan." He gulped for air.

She dragged in a breath. "What plan?"

"I didn't tell you?"

"Don't think so. I might have missed it though. I get distracted when you're kissing and fondling me."

"And once I get started..." His chest heaved. "I need to get out of here, though. The later I arrive at the bunkhouse to shower and change, the more the story falls apart. Lingering here is suspicious."

"I'm still unclear about the story."

"Sorry." He raked his fingers through his hair and cleared his throat. "I figured we'd tell folks we're using this time to work on our friendship."

She smiled. "Okay."

"You don't think they'll buy it?"

He was adorable. "No, but it's worth a try."

"It's the truth, in a way."

"How are we working on it? I mean, other than knocking boots all night, which we won't mention."

"We'll spend the day taking the same trail ride we went on in August. It's a do-over, to get rid of any remaining negativity."

"Didn't we get rid of it last night? I could've sworn between round two and three, the negativity just—"

"They don't know that."

"Right. Not telling. Got it."

"The concept of repeating that ride and ending the day friends instead of enemies will appeal to them. You'll see."

"If you can sell that story, I'll back you up."

"It will buy us a day to ourselves."

"But I seriously doubt they'll be fooled about last night."

He gazed at her. "And maybe that's okay. I just want to set some boundaries. The Brotherhood knows I brought condoms over here. They don't need to know we used them."

"I'm with you, cowboy." She glanced toward the window. "Sun's coming up. I'll text Henri, let her know about the ride and check on Aunt Lilith."

"Can you believe I forgot all about your aunt?"

"I'd like to forget about her."

"Can we even go on this ride? Or do you have to babysit her?"

"Henri has babysitting duty today. She insisted on it after Aunt Lilith maneuvered us into taking her home."

He let out a sigh of relief. "That's awesome. I'll figure out some way to thank her later."

She nodded. "Me, too. Lots of ways."

"Then we're all set. Would you be willing to pack a lunch?"

"Be happy to. Should I bring it to the barn?"

"Tell you what. I'll saddle the horses and ride over here. Do you want Lucky Ducky again?"

"Absolutely. I love that horse. When should I be ready?"

"How does an hour sound?"

"Great. What are you going to do about breakfast?"

"I'll grab a bowl of cereal at the bunkhouse."

She made a face. "I could make you something quick before you leave."

"I couldn't handle it."

"Your stomach's upset?"

"My stomach's fine. It's the area below my belt that's the problem. It wants what it wants, and it's not breakfast."

"Oh." Her core tightened. "Ever hear of a quickie?"

"Yes, ma'am."

"Want to do that?"

"Yes, ma'am." He stood. "Can't risk it."

"Why?"

"I'd still be wearing a big ol' smile when I walked into that bunkhouse. The truth would be written all over my face."

27

Beautiful day. Beautiful woman to share it with. Rafe couldn't ask for more as he and Kate ambled down the trail side-by-side on Butch and Lucky Ducky.

Two months ago the weather had been hot and Kate's mood had been cool. Today the weather was cool and Kate was looking hot. He'd brought a blanket and tied it behind his saddle. Spread out, it had more square footage than a double bed.

As they'd mounted up in front of her cottage and started toward the trail, she'd offered to cook dinner for him tonight. That would be a treat.

The real treat would be after dinner, though. He'd be wise not to dwell on that, but he wasn't wise when it came to Kate. This time there'd be no party at the fire pit, no doubt about whether he'd share her bed.

The guys had given him knowing smiles when he'd spun his yarn about friendship this morning. But they hadn't called bullshit. Tomorrow they might. So what? After two nights of making sweet love to Kate he'd be so high he wouldn't give a damn about anything. He'd brought his razor this time so he could—

"I talked to Aunt Lilith this morning."

"Oh?" The sensual movie rolling in his head switched over to something that featured screeching violins. "And?"

"She and Henri were having breakfast when I texted, so she knew I was up and she called me."

"How's she doing?" He didn't care, but Kate's tone put him on alert. She'd brought this up for a reason.

She gazed straight ahead. "She's excited because the Babes invited her to be part of their monthly sleepover tonight."

"Tonight?"

She turned to look at him. "Weird, right?"

"On so many levels. It's not the right day. They always do it on Thursday nights. And they don't even like her."

"I know. She's going to be with Henri all day so I couldn't figure out how to talk to Henri and ask what's going on. Aunt Lilith said they switched the night so she could be there. She's totally flattered."

"They're up to something. They don't invite just anybody to those sleepovers. You have to be a barrel racer and have a buckskin, for one thing."

"They've invited Ellie Mae Stockton, too. She's driving up from Eagles Nest today. She doesn't fit the profile, either."

"She doesn't, but she makes better sense than your aunt. Ellie Mae endeared herself to the

Babes during the bachelor auction. Your aunt's a pain in the butt."

"So maybe they switched nights to accommodate Ellie Mae, and Aunt Lilith just happens to be here, although that's not the way she presented it."

"It could be the only night Ellie Mae could get away, since she works at the drugstore down there. It is the right week, at least. I can see Lilith wanting to believe the timing was all about her, though."

"Which it still could be. She's flying out tomorrow."

His stomach clenched. She'd known that factoid since he'd arrived with Butch and Lucky. Should have been the first thing she said when she saw him. "Kind of buried the lead, there, Kate."

She sighed. "Yes, I did. It caught me off guard. I expected she'd stay a few more days."

"I thought you wanted her out of here ASAP."

"That was before... before we..."

"Yeah, okay." He got it. Her plan to quit while they were ahead remained firmly in place. But now that they'd done the deed, she'd hoped for an extension on the timeline.

"It's not like she has a job she has to rush back to. She seemed intrigued with the ranch and she likes you a lot."

"Then why's she leaving?"

"She's attending a gala next weekend and she's spending three days in Chicago with her friends dress shopping."

"Of course she is." He took a deep breath. "Tomorrow, huh?"

"Tomorrow."

"I seem to recall you were the one who decided we'd end this when she left. It's a free country. You can change your mind."

"It makes the most sense, though." Once again she stared straight ahead, her back straight as a ruler. "We weren't supposed to be in this situation in the first place. It's better if we end it cleanly when she leaves."

"Cleanly?" He had internal bleeding. Nothing clean about that.

"You know what I mean."

"No, Kate, I don't. You may be able to make a clean cut and go on, but—"

"You said you'd take the deal."

Yep. He'd have said anything for the privilege of making love to her. But he was a man of his word. If he'd given it in haste, if he'd given it because he'd counted on changing her mind, then he'd gambled and lost. Nudging back his hat, he gazed at the fall foliage decorating the slopes of the mountains. Breathtaking scenery. Didn't help.

"You're upset."

He looked at her. "Like you're not?"

"Maybe we need to figure out how to lessen the impact."

"I didn't bring any booze."

"Ah, Rafe. Only you could make me smile at a time like this."

"That's because I'm a keeper."

"Yes, you are."

"So keep me."

"No can do. I'm putting you back."

"This bites, Kate."

"I know. I'm sorry." Her expression softened. "Listen, maybe we shouldn't drag this out. You could leave your truck in front of the cottage tonight and walk back to the bunkhouse. If she's partying with the Babes, she'll never know you didn't stay overnight."

The ache in his chest made breathing tough. "Is that what you want?"

She held his gaze. "I was the kid who begged to stay until the park closed. My folks wanted to leave early because of traffic. I hated getting stuck in traffic, too, but it was worth it for one more roller coaster ride."

He swallowed.

"But you may prefer leaving early to avoid the traffic."

If she could take it, he could take it. "We'll stay in the park until it closes."

"Okay."

He surveyed the trail ahead. "There's a clearing about half a mile from here. It's off the trail a couple hundred feet. Want to stop there?"

"Instead of going all the way to the glen?"

"Uh-huh."

"Is it as pretty as the glen?"

"No, but it's a lot closer. And more private."

"Gotcha. The clearing it is."

* * *

Rafe sat on the blanket, cross-legged and barefoot, his shirt unbuttoned as he ate the turkey sandwich Kate had made. "This tastes good."

"Thanks." She sat across from him wearing her jeans and her shirt. She'd left her bra off and her shirt unbuttoned at his request. "Glad you like it."

"I like the way you taste even better."

She blushed, and the rosy color moved from her cheeks to her throat and down to the swell of her breasts. "I've never done that in the great outdoors."

"Was it better or worse?"

"Better. I was one with nature. Or maybe it was great because you're talented. It might be equally nice indoors."

"I enjoyed having more room to work." He polished off the sandwich and took a long pull on his bottle of virgin cider.

"I brought brownies for dessert."

"Excellent choice. But let's hold off." He finished his cider and put the bottle in the grass. "I'd like it very much if you'd take off your jeans and panties again."

She grinned. "Give me one good reason."

"Glad to." He stood, fished a condom out of his pocket and unzipped his jeans. "One good reason coming up. And I do mean *up*."

She sucked in a breath. "Happy to comply." She laid back on the blanket and wiggled out of her clothes. "Was that fast enough?"

"Almost." He moved between her open thighs. Bracing himself above her, he leaned down and brushed a kiss over her mouth, rosy from his kisses. "I didn't check the ground for stones before

I spread out the blanket. If one starts digging into you, stop me." He probed once and thrust into her warmth.

She moaned softly.

"Feel a stone?"

"I feel you. That blocks out everything else."

Lifting his head, he gazed into her luminescent gray eyes as he began to stroke. "This just gets better and better."

"Is it because…"

"The clock's ticking?"

"Yeah."

"Could be." He picked up the pace. "Stay with me, Kate. It's roller-coaster time."

28

As Kate guided Lucky Ducky over to the hitching post in front of the barn, she glanced at Rafe. "Leo's bringing in the horses from the pasture. Tell me the truth, do I look ravished?"

"A little bit. Do I?"

"A little bit. Leo will know exactly what—"

"He'll also know we had fun. He'd rather see that than sad faces. Or angry ones."

"You're right. The gang's had enough of that from us. I plan to do better."

"Me, too." He swung down from the saddle. "I'll fetch the halters and lead ropes."

"Thanks." She dismounted as Leo arrived leading Prince and Thunder. "Hey, Leo."

"Hey, Kate." Leo paused, the corners of his mouth twitching as if he wanted to grin. "How was the ride?"

"Excellent, thanks. Gorgeous weather."

"Sure was. One of the guests mentioned seeing a couple of bears yesterday in the glen where you were headed. Any sign of them?"

"Didn't notice any." She managed to say it with a straight face.

He ducked his head, but not fast enough to hide his grin. "That's good."

"Do you have any info on why the Babes are having a sleepover tonight?"

When he glanced up, he was in control of himself again. "Only that it's happening and we're all thinking what the hell. Makes no sense."

"Did they switch days because Ellie Mae gets Sunday off?"

"Possibly, although why not move it ahead to next Sunday when your aunt's gone?"

"That would be logical, wouldn't it? They must be up to something."

"That's a given." Prince gave him a nudge. "Somebody's impatient for his dinner. If you'll excuse me, I'd better get these guys inside. Glad your ride went well." He led the horses into the barn and exchanged a few words with Rafe as they passed each other.

She took the halter and rope Rafe handed her. "Leo said someone's seen bears in the glen. He wondered if we'd come across any sign of them."

"What did you say?"

"That we didn't notice anything."

"Good answer."

"The Brotherhood doesn't know why the Babes switched their sleepover, either."

"Then for sure they have something up their sleeve. Need any help with anything?"

"No, thanks. I've been working on my horse skills recently."

"Oh, yeah?" He smiled. "Then I'll try not to get in your way."

They worked in silence for several minutes as Leo came and went, returning horses to the barn two at a time. When she lifted off the saddle ready to carry it inside, Rafe stood holding his saddle, clearly waiting for her to finish. "You didn't have to wait for me."

"I've enjoyed watching you. You weren't kidding about your skills. You know your way around the leather." He tilted his head to indicate she should go ahead of him.

"I've spent a fair amount of time at the barn the past couple of months."

"How did I miss that?"

"I got the schedule from Henri and picked hours you'd be elsewhere."

"I see. Who was teaching you?"

"Henri. I tried to pay her but she said this was a perk of working here and now she had another capable hand if she needed one."

"I sure hope you'll stop avoiding me."

"I will." She went into the tack room and returned the saddle to its stand.

"If you're making time to come down to the barn, maybe we could schedule a ride now and then."

"I'd like that." She picked up the grooming tote and glanced at him before heading out of the barn. "But we might have to wait a while."

He followed her out. "How long do you suppose we'll have to wait?"

"I don't know." She put down the tote so they could both reach it, grabbed a brush and started working on Lucky with firm, quick strokes.

"I'm sure there will come a time when we can be together and not—"

"I can't picture it." The rhythm of his brush strokes matched hers. He lowered his voice as Leo went through the barn door with the last two from the pasture. "That's what's hanging me up. Now I know what making love to you feels like. It's in my mind, in my body, in my blood. I can't imagine those urges going away."

"Because you're too close to it. When you get some distance, you'll—"

"What distance?" He moved to Butch's far side. "Your friends are mine, and vice versa. We'll see each other every day. If you stop avoiding me, we'll meet here at the barn. You've already agreed to play poker at the bunkhouse. We'll—"

"Stop." She dragged in a breath. "You're freaking me out."

"Sorry." He tossed the brush in the tote and took out a rag to wipe Butch's coat. "I think I'm doing okay and then I..." He shook his head. "I want to believe we can go from lovers to friends. Other people do it, right?"

"I don't know anybody personally." She began wiping Lucky's coat, too. "But you see it all the time on TV."

"Well, then. We'll just follow the same script as characters on TV. What could go wrong?"

"Sarcasm doesn't become you."

He sighed. "And it's not how I want to talk to you. I apologize. Again."

"Apology accepted." She gave Lucky one last swipe with the rag and turned. "Seriously, you don't have to stay until the park closes. I'm not a kid anymore."

Nudging back his hat, he gazed at her. "Maybe I am."

"What if the Tilt-a-Whirl makes you sick to your stomach?"

"I won't let that happen."

"I wish I believed you. Just drive me back to the cottage, park the truck in front and sneak out the back."

"Sneaking out the back is not my style." His jaw firmed. "And neither is complaining about getting stuck in traffic. That ends now. It's party time."

* * *

Rafe made good on his vow. Fixing dinner became an adventure punctuated with many kiss breaks. One of those got out of hand when he hoisted her to the kitchen counter and made love to her while the country fries burned to a crisp.

The chicken breasts were overdone, too, and the salad looked like it had been thrown together. Because it had.

"I'm embarrassed about this meal," she said as they finally sat at the kitchen table with a couple bottles of cider. "It's not my best effort."

"I don't know what you're talking about." He dug into the blackened potatoes. "Eating these reminds me of making you come. The chicken is overcooked because I had my hands under your shirt. We made the salad together between bouts of kissing. This is the sexiest dinner I've ever had. Eat up. You'll need your strength for later."

"I have an idea for later."

"Good. I have several ideas. Let's share."

"What if we drag both mattresses out to the living room and push them together?"

"How about I carry them out so I can flex my muscles?"

"So you like the idea?"

"Sure do. The extra width would be awesome, especially if we can figure out how to keep them together. I don't want to lose you in the crack."

"I have a solution so they won't slide. We put one up against the hearth, set the other one beside it and push the couch over to hold them in place."

"That could work."

"It'll still be too short for you, but better than what we've dealt with. What you require is a super king, or whatever the biggest bed is called."

"It's called Rafe's custom-made bed and someday I'll have one."

"I'm sure you will." And just like that, they'd fallen into the trap of looking ahead instead of focusing on the present. She took a breath. "Let's go get those mattresses."

29

The flash of sadness in Kate's eyes frustrated the hell out of Rafe. How could he convince her to take a chance on him? He didn't give a damn about that custom bed unless she was in it with him.

But he couldn't say that or they'd be right back in the weeds. He pushed away from the table. "Maybe we should put the dishes in a sink full of soapy water before we—" The sounds of multiple horns honking shattered the stillness of the night. "What the devil is that?"

"The Babes are here."

"Here? In front of the cottage? Dear God, I hope they're not staging a chivaree."

"What's a chivaree?"

"It's when people gather outside the house of newlyweds to make a ruckus banging on pots and pans. I haven't heard of using car horns, but there's no reason that wouldn't be—"

"They're up at Henri's, not down here. It just sounds like they're right outside. They did the same thing last time."

"Why, for Pete's sake?"

"It's their new thing."

"I don't remember hearing this kind of racket before last month's sleepover."

"Maybe you were inside with music on. It was just like this. Even louder. They might have decided to keep it down because you're here."

"Sounds doggone loud to me. Ah, good. They've stopped. What's the deal?"

"Red thought they needed some sort of official salute to begin the proceedings. She wanted a line of trumpets, but nobody at the Buckskin plays the trumpet."

"I'm sure they could find a recorded fanfare they could use."

"It was considered. Nobody liked the idea. They wanted it to be live. They chose the horns on their vehicles."

"Did they warn you ahead of time?"

She smiled. "They did better than that. They asked my permission, since I'd be the main one affected. It's once a month, so I said sure. I wonder what Aunt Lilith thought of it."

"A few honking car horns is nothing to what she's in for once the party gets started."

"And that's why I wear my earplugs during their sleepovers. Especially after they bought the karaoke machine."

"Did you hear about the bawdy songs Ed loaded on that thing?"

"Oh, my God. Aunt Lilith will flip out."

"Ed added the songs after that hair salon party she staged for Ellie Mae a few days after the auction. She and Ellie Mae know all the words and the others wanted to learn them."

"No wonder Ellie Mae's driving up. She and Ed make quite a... wait, that's it! I know why they rescheduled. They want to gross out Aunt Lilith with bawdy karaoke and drunken hijinks so she won't ever come back."

Rafe gazed at her. "She does seem to like the place a little too much."

"She also thinks you're terrific. With what she's seen so far, she'll have charming stories to tell her friends about her niece and the hunky cowboy. Then she'll need to fly back to gather more charming stories."

"And if she's dropped comments to Henri about future visits..."

"Henri would pull out all the stops to keep her away."

"Then I hope it works. That's assuming you don't want more visits from dear Aunt Lilith." More visits would mean more cottage time for him, but he wouldn't point that out, either. So many land mines.

Kate met his gaze. "I can't imagine what that would be like, having her fly out at a moment's notice, which is what she loves doing."

"Disruptive." And he'd take it in a heartbeat if it meant he could spend the nights here.

"We won't have to worry about it, though. The Babes have appointed themselves guardians of the Buckskin."

"As usual." Kate was probably right. The Babes were nothing if not thorough. Lilith wouldn't be coming back. "Well, mystery solved. We can forget about their sleepover." He stood and pulled her to her feet. "And concentrate on ours."

* * *

Making love when time was running out added intensity, but Rafe would trade it instantly for a lifetime of everyday married sex with Kate. She wasn't giving him that option.

She lay on her side facing him, eyes closed, pale lashes fluttering as she dreamed. She'd fallen asleep while insisting she wasn't tired. As she'd drifted off, she'd stroked his thigh and claimed she had lots of energy left. A little catnap was all she needed.

One more time, Rafe. Her hand still rested on his thigh. It twitched as her muscles relaxed. Her tousled curls bore testimony to their last round. Around three they'd showered together, dried off and come back to bed because she'd wanted to treat him to oral sex, but not in the slippery shower.

What a treat it had been, too. As she'd driven him crazy, he'd managed to keep from coming by stroking his fingers through her hair, over and over.

When he was on the brink, he'd made her stop so he could suit up and sink into her warm body once more. Could be for the last time. They'd been arguing that point when she'd dozed off.

The lights were still on all over the house. They'd drawn the curtains so they could roam freely without getting dressed. A two-person orgy.

He'd learned where she loved to be stroked and where she was ticklish. She'd mapped the same territory on him. They'd made a lot of noise.

Oddly enough, he hadn't heard much from Henri's place. Some music and laughter had spilled out, but not at the volume the Babes were famous for. Now, as dawn approached, everything was quiet in the big house.

Here, too. Gave him time to count his blessings. He wouldn't get what he wanted, but thanks to Lilith he'd been allowed this chance to hold Kate in his arms and kiss her with all the love in his heart. He'd spent hours caressing her silken skin and giving her pleasure.

She'd returned the favor, welcoming him and responding with such eagerness that he'd had the most satisfying orgasms of his life. These intimate moments with Kate would sustain him. He had much to be grateful for. He would always—

"Hey." She followed her low, sexy murmur with a lazy caress, smoothing her hand up his thigh and over his hip. "I'm awake."

Fire shot through his veins as he looked into her eyes. No mistaking what the lady wanted. "I see that."

"One more time?"

His heart hammered as he reached blindly for the condom packets scattered on the hearth. "You don't even have to ask."

"Yes, I do. You might be too tired."

He smiled. "No, ma'am."

"Your friend says the same thing."

He glanced down as she wrapped her hand around his rapidly expanding cock. Her ring hand.

Would she take her ring off today? He handed her the packet. "Want to put it on?" *One last time.*

"Yes." She let go of him so she could rip open the package. Tossing the wrapper over her shoulder, she lovingly rolled on the condom. The turquoise and malachite set into her ring caught the light. "There."

"Any special requests?"

"No." She stretched out on her back, her head on a pillow. "This is my favorite."

"Mine, too." He moved over her, braced on his forearms.

She slid her palms up his chest and wound her arms around his neck. "Thank you."

"Don't thank me yet." He gradually slid his cock into her tight channel as he held her gaze. "I'm not done."

Her breath caught. "I meant for... everything."

"Loved those burnt potatoes, did you?" He began an easy rhythm.

"Yes."

"And the bruise on your tush from the rock under the blanket?" He picked up the pace.

"Uh-huh." Her breasts quivered as she gulped in air. "Badge of honor."

"And when we got so wild we shoved the mattresses apart?"

"Didn't feel a thing. Too busy coming."

"Same here." And he would soon do that again. She was close and he was right behind her.

"Everything, Rafe." She gripped his shoulders. "Loved it all."

"I love you."

She swallowed. "I love you, too."

"It's forever, Kate." He thrust harder. "I'll always love you."

She started to shake her head.

"You know it's true. You *know*." He pushed deep and she came.

She gasped, but didn't cry out. Her turbulent gaze locked with his and her fingers dug into his shoulders as she arched into her release.

With a groan, he slipped the leash on his control, shaking violently as the climax rocked him from the roots of his hair to the tips of his toes. As he absorbed the aftershocks, his and hers, he searched her stormy gray eyes for a glimpse of a possible future. He couldn't give up. Not yet.

He'd put all he had into loving her. Had it been enough? There. A glimmer.

Then she closed her eyes.

_30_

Kate had set her alarm since she was due at the dining hall to cook breakfast. But the click of the front door closing woke her before the alarm chimed.

Rafe had turned off the lights they'd left on all night, so the house was cloaked in early morning shadows. As she sat up, a piece of paper fluttered on the pillow next to hers.

Rafe's note was short. His bold handwriting barely fit on the scrap of paper he'd found, a receipt from the Apple Barrel General Store that she'd left in the kitchen. _Barn duty. Leave mattresses for me. Love, Rafe_

She located her phone on the coffee table and checked the time. She'd have to leave the mattresses, either for him to move or for her to wrestle out of here when she came back. Showering and dressing would take all the time she had before heading to the dining hall.

As she hurried through her routine, the bare box springs on her bed kept Rafe front and center, darn it. She didn't want him there. She wanted him tucked away until she'd had coffee and a chance to gather her wits.

She snatched up her phone on the way out the door. A text from Henri. She pocketed the phone and left. No time, now. She left the door unlocked in case Rafe came back to move the mattresses.

The parking area next to Henri's was empty. The Babes had left. When had Aunt Lilith planned to fly out? Lack of sleep and lots of sex had blurred that detail.

The dining hall kitchen looked the same as it had the last time she'd cooked a meal here on Friday night, less than forty-eight hours ago. How was that possible?

With a sense of relief, she threw herself into preparing the meal. She sipped coffee to jumpstart her brain as she worked. Greeting the guests who arrived eager for breakfast helped, too. Feeding people gave her joy.

Toward the end of the breakfast hour, Henri showed up in the dining hall looking surprisingly chipper after a sleepover with the Babes. Normally a Babes pajama party meant a morning hangover.

Kate gave her a smile and a hug. "Do you want breakfast? I still have—"

"No, thanks. Some coffee is fine. I can get it."

"Don't drink what's in the coffee urn. It's been there a while. I'll get you some fresh."

"Okay. After everyone clears out, we need to talk. I texted you, but I—"

"I haven't had time to read it."

"Doesn't matter. I just asked you to call me when you had a minute. After I thought about it, I decided to come over here and talk to you in person."

"Then I'll be right back with your coffee." Returning to the kitchen, she poured coffee into a Buckskin logo mug and walked into the dining room as the last couple was going out the door. "Have a nice day, folks!" she called after them.

"We will! Thanks, Kate!" They gave her a wave.

Henri watched the interchange with a smile. "We get such nice people here."

"Mostly." Kate set down the coffee in front of Henri before taking a seat across from her.

She laughed. "Right. Want to get some coffee?"

"Thanks, but I've been sipping while I cooked. I'm good. You're looking great, by the way."

Henri gave her an amused glance. "As opposed to the way I usually am after a Babes sleepover?"

"Well..."

"It's okay. I know I usually look like hell after partying with the Babes. But this time we didn't get drunk and disorderly. We might have to remedy that by scheduling another sleepover on Thursday. To celebrate our win."

"I'm so confused. I thought your plan was to shock the pants off Aunt Lilith."

"We did think of that." Henri sipped her coffee. "But Ed came up with a better plan. We decided to stay relatively sober and get Lilith smashed."

"Are we talking blackmail pictures?"

"No, but that was on the table for a while. A very short while." She drank more coffee. "You can get arrested for blackmailing someone."

"What did you do?"

"We got her tipsy on her Dom Perignon while Ed dispensed financial advice. We acted like the advice was for Ellie Mae, but our target was Lilith."

"Why? She has plenty of money."

"And isn't the least bit savvy about managing it. She pays through the nose for taxes. We hauled out my laptop and convinced her she needed to set up the Lilith Cutler Foundation for Aspiring Medical Practitioners to save tax dollars."

"Medical practitioners like Ginny?"

"Oh, Ginny's just the beginning. She's fully funded, by the way. All the way to graduation. Ed set it up using Lilith's banking info. We have account numbers, routing numbers, the works. She's so easy when she's drunk."

"Can she reverse it when she's sober?"

"Nope. For one thing, she doesn't fully understand how to administer it, so Ed's doing that for her. Pro bono, of course."

Kate clapped her hands together. "I can't freaking believe this! It's fabulous! Aunt Lilith's money will finally be used for good. Ginny's education is paid for? All of it?"

"All of it."

She gazed at Henri, her throat tightening. "How can I ever thank you? Or Ed? Or the Babes for orchestrating this?"

"Brownies are always welcome."

"I'll start baking."

Henri reached across the table and took her hand. "Seriously, you don't have to do anything. This was a sucky situation and we found a way to make it right."

"Is Aunt Lilith still here?"

"Her chauffeur picked her up about thirty minutes ago. She was in no shape to see anyone. Hangover city."

"I guess I should feel sorry for her."

"No, you shouldn't. She's still selfish and manipulative. We preyed on her weakness, a desire to be admired. We told her this foundation would generate publicity. Lucy's our PR expert. She's going to contact some people in Indianapolis and get Lilith's new venture some airtime."

"I'm in awe. You guys rock."

"By the way, have you called your mom and Ginny to tell them about the wedding?"

"No. I meant to do it yesterday, but—"

"Yesterday didn't go according to plan."

Her cheeks warmed. "No."

"I guess it's better that you haven't called them. There's one other aspect of this. It might not have occurred to you yet, but it's something to consider."

"What's that?"

"Ginny's education is assured. Your marriage to Rafe is no longer necessary." She hesitated. "I don't know where you are in your thinking, but if you wish, you can start divorce proceedings anytime you choose."

Her joy curdled in her stomach, leaving her feeling queasy. "Uh, that's true, I guess. Since it's only been a couple of days, maybe an annulment would—"

"I thought that, too, but after Lilith tottered off to bed, we discussed it. With their multiple marriages, Ed and Ellie Mae are experts on the subject. They said an annulment is way more complicated than a divorce."

"Really? I figured it would be easier." And less traumatic.

"Evidently not. For one thing, you have to testify that the marriage was not consummated."

She fought the urge to cover her hot face. "Wow. That sounds so—"

"Outdated? Invasive? I know." Henri's sympathetic gaze held hers. "If you need help with this, let me know."

She swallowed. "Thank you."

* * *

Rafe's truck was parked in front of the cottage when Kate came home after cleaning up the dining hall and kitchen. He was the last person she wanted to deal with right now, and yet the one person who deserved to have the information from Henri ASAP. He was, at least for now, her lawfully wedded husband.

He'd already moved her mattress back to her bedroom by the time she walked in and he was coming out to pick up the one that belonged in Millie's room. He didn't look surprised to see her.

She paused just inside the doorway. "Hi." His hat and keys lay on the table next to it. She was used to seeing them there.

"Hi." He took a breath. "I was hoping you'd come back while I was doing this. I hated leaving without saying goodbye, but you needed the sleep, so I—"

"I understand."

"Let me get this other mattress transferred and maybe we can take a minute to talk. I have a little time before I have to head back to the barn."

"Okay." She took off her jacket and laid it over the back of the couch, which was still out of position. Unless he'd loaded the dishwasher, their dishes from last night were in the sink. Condom packets lay on the hearth.

He picked up the second mattress as if it weighed nothing and carried it into Millie's old room. And looked damned good doing it.

She was hungry, exhausted and torn between elation for Ginny and dread about how Rafe would react to talk of divorce. "I'm grabbing some brownies. Want some?"

"Always!" he called back.

"I'll make coffee."

"Great!"

She had coffee brewing when he walked into the kitchen. She turned toward him. "I saw Henri this—"

"Never mind about Henri." He eliminated the space between them and pulled her close. "I didn't get to kiss you good morning." He dipped his head and took firm possession of her mouth.

What was happening? Lilith was gone, which meant she and Rafe were... She lost her place as the warmth of his kiss drove out everything else. She clung to him—solid, loving, kind. Rafe.

He released her slowly and smiled. "That's better."

"Yeah." She let out a breath. "The brownies are in the fridge. I'll pour coffee if you'll—"

"I'm on it. Want to sit on the porch?"

"Sure. The living room's still jacked up." And fresh air might clear her head and organize her jumbled thoughts.

"Jacked up in a good cause." He opened the refrigerator door and took out the brownies. "I didn't attempt to remake the beds."

"That's fine. I'll handle it." The coffeemaker shut off. "Coffee's ready."

He handed her the container of brownies. "I'll get it. Go have a seat. You look stressed."

"And here I thought I was projecting calm confidence."

"Might work with people who don't know you very well. Won't fly with me. See you on the porch."

She carried the brownies outside and took the far chair, the one he'd sat in Saturday morning when he'd wanted to revisit the idea of having an affair—while they were married.

He shouldered his way out the screen door holding both mugs of coffee, glanced at her and smiled. "You took my chair."

"Felt like it."

"Alrighty, then." He handed over her coffee.

"Thanks."

He settled into the other one. "How do you like the view from there?"

"It's different. I never sit here. When Millie and I lived together, she liked this chair. It's angled more toward the road so you can see who's coming. Mine's angled toward the trees."

"Millie likes to be notified in advance."

"So do you."

"Yes, ma'am. Millie and I share that."

"Jumping into this marriage with no notice must have torqued you something fierce."

He sipped his coffee. "Hasn't been the easiest thing, but I wouldn't trade a minute of it."

He hadn't picked up a brownie. She glanced at the container. "Aren't you going to have one?"

"This discussion of chair positions makes me think I'd better hold off until you say your piece. Don't want to choke on a bite of brownie."

"Fair enough." She set down her coffee and scooted around in her chair. "Last night the Babes, mostly Ed, talked Aunt Lilith into setting up an educational foundation. Ginny's the first recipient and now she has a full ride."

"Wow. That's terrific." His gaze met hers. "Can Lilith reverse it?"

"I asked Henri the same thing. Ed set it up so that once the money goes out, there's no getting it back."

He went very quiet. Using great care, he set his coffee on the side table. "So you don't need me anymore?"

31

"That's a terrible way to put it." Kate's brow furrowed. "Of course I—"

"It's accurate, though." He was supposed to have years to prepare for this. Years to try staving it off, somehow. But here it was, gut-punching him with a force that left him stunned and disoriented.

"I have a thought."

Hope kindled a tiny flame. He cleared his throat. "What's that?"

"We go ahead with the divorce, but..."

The flame went out. He looked away.

"We continue to see each other."

He could be a smartass. Ask her what *continue to see each other* meant. Make her spell it out. Undoubtedly there would be rules and regs. He wouldn't live here. He'd just drop by for sex now and then.

God, he was tempted. But he'd had a taste of how it could be. He wanted that. He wouldn't settle. Not anymore.

"What do you think?"

He tugged off his ring and laid it gently on the table. "Sorry, Kate. That won't work for me." He stood, ducked inside and grabbed his hat and keys.

A quick exit was best. He'd get out of there before he said or did something that would ruin their friendship. Again. They'd promised the gang that wouldn't happen.

* * *

Two hellish days later, Rafe had only glimpsed Kate from a distance. A blessing and a curse. The Brotherhood had offered comfort in the form of hard cider and hard labor. He'd gone easy on the booze. He'd been down that road two months ago and it wasn't the answer.

But he'd gladly accepted the job of mucking out the stalls every day. Nothing like it to power through bouts of anger and frustration. If he was still shoveling horse poop by Christmas, so what?

It was the perfect assignment for a shitty situation and he was grateful. Most cowboys found satisfaction in the task, so the Brotherhood was doing him a favor. In return he'd promised not to repeat the sulky behavior he'd indulged in last time he'd been crossways with Kate.

He'd kept that promise, delivering such a wagonload of good cheer the Brotherhood had warned him to tone it down or they'd punch him in his constantly smiling face. Sadly for them, he had only two settings these days. They wouldn't want to see the alternate one, so they were stuck with his clenched-jaw grin.

If he could maintain it through tonight's poker game, he was awarding himself an Oscar. Kate would be there.

Nick arrived early and asked Rafe to come outside and evaluate his truck's aging fuel pump.

Rafe played along and followed him to the parking area. "You don't have a fuel pump issue, do you?"

"Not anymore. Replaced it last week." Nick leaned against the front fender. "Just need to know the lay of the land. Has she filed yet?"

"Not that I know of."

"Is tonight your first face-to-face since Monday?"

"Yep."

"I'm a little surprised she agreed to come."

"I am, too. Then again, how else can we make sure this doesn't blow a hole in the group like it did last time? She needs to feel free to play poker like she used to, and I need to be fine with that."

"Are you?"

"I have to be."

"But *are* you?"

He sighed. "What do you think? I love her. I want to spend the rest of my days with her. She doesn't feel the same. That hurts like hell."

"She's into you, though. She wasn't pretending to kiss you at the wedding. She meant it."

"But she doesn't trust me. Not enough to go all-in. I want that trust from her, bro. I need it."

"Yeah, you do. I wouldn't have understood it before, but now, with Eva, I—" The deep rumble of a Ford 350 signaled Jake's truck was on the way. "He's gonna play?"

"Yep. Bringing Millie, too. And Kate. They fetched her from the dining hall." His gut tightened.

Nick glanced in the direction of the bobbing headlights on the bumpy road. "Makes sense that Millie came to give Kate support. Want to head inside?"

"No, I'll stay out here to welcome her. It's the classy thing to do."

"Want me to go inside?"

"I could use some support, too."

"You've got it."

"You could open your hood, though, and act like we have a reason to be out here."

"Sure thing. Got your phone?"

"Yeah." He pulled it out while Nick propped open the hood of his vintage truck.

"Shine your flashlight on the innards. We'll act like we're checking the fuel pump."

Rafe trained his phone flashlight under the hood. "Damn, it's so *clean* under here."

"A clean engine is a happy engine."

"So where are Eva and her friends having their girls' night?"

"Fiona's apartment."

"I don't get Fiona. Why bid so much on Leo and call it quits after one date? He's a great guy."

"Freaks her out that he's so handsome."

"Huh?"

"Don't say anything. It's not like he can ugly up and solve that problem." He pushed away from the grill of the truck. "Douse your light. They're here." He lowered the hood with a clang.

The night was cool, but sweat ran down Rafe's spine as he pasted on a smile and turned toward the incoming truck. Jake slowly backed in, putting the passenger side facing Rafe and Nick.

"I'll get Millie." Nick moved toward the front passenger door as Jake cut the engine. "Kate's all yours."

If only. Would she see him approaching and head out the other side? He reached for the back door at the same moment she opened it. He gulped. "Hey."

"Hey." Her smile looked fake, too.

He offered his hand and she put a container of brownies into it. He shifted them to his other hand, but by then she was down. "I'm glad you decided to come." He handed her the brownies.

"Had to," she murmured, holding the container with both hands. Her left ring finger was bare. "We can't let things get weird."

"Right." She'd taken off her ring. Made his chest hurt, but why wouldn't she? He had. Red had trusted in the energy of those stones. He'd wanted her to be right.

Kate glanced up at him, her expression achingly vulnerable. "It's weird, anyway."

The stones hadn't worked if she was divorcing him. But at least she wasn't divorcing the group. He dug deep for some reassuring words to help her through tonight. "No worries, Kate. You've got this."

"And brownies." She gave him a tiny smile, a real one this time. "Come on, Millie. Let's show these boys how it's done." She started toward the bunkhouse.

Jake came around the truck. "Got a problem, Nick? Saw you and Rafe checking out your truck."

"Just showing him the fuel pump I installed last week."

"Uh-huh." Jake waited until Kate and Millie were inside. "This is going to be weird, isn't it?"

"Not if I can help it." Rafe glanced at him. "How's she doing?"

"Putting on a show, just like you."

"This first time will be the worst," Nick said. "It'll get better."

Jake nodded. "It will. An intimate little poker game tonight, chuck wagon stew out by the fire pit Friday night. Before you know it, we'll be hanging out at the Moose, faking it there, too."

Nick snorted.

"Fake it 'til you make it, right, bro?" Rafe smiled at Jake.

He shrugged. "Always worked for me."

"It was good of Millie to come."

"Never any doubt she would once Kate said she was doing it. Millie's here to be the bridge over troubled waters."

"That's Millie for you," Nick said. "Fighting to keep the old gang together."

"We'll have no troubled waters." Rafe squared his shoulders. "I'll make sure of it." He started toward the bunkhouse. "Let's play some poker."

As he walked, he reached into his pocket for the smooth hematite Red had given him. Several times in the past two days he'd started to throw it into the woods. But Red had told him it aided soldiers wounded in battle. He'd hang onto it a little longer.

32

"And I win again!" Kate scooped the chips in with both hands and began sorting them. "Thank you all for your contributions." How ironic that on a night when she didn't give a damn about winning, she couldn't lose.

"You're welcome," Jake said. "I'm sure Millie won't mind if I don't buy her the strings of pumpkin lights she wants for the front porch."

"Don't let him con you." Millie gave Jake a nudge. "I bought those lights and they'll be here this week. Jake's ego has taken a bigger hit than his pocketbook."

"Yeah, man up, dude." Leo swept a hand over his meager supply of chips. "She's almost cleaned me out, too."

"Kate's a savvy player," Rafe said. "Underestimate her at your peril. I learned that the hard way."

She glanced at him. Did his comment have a double meaning, a barbed comment on their jacked-up relationship? Instead his expression held nothing but kindness and admiration. "Thanks, Rafe."

He touched two fingers to the brim of his hat and smiled. Several of the guys wore their hats when they played, claiming it brought them luck. The brim also allowed them to duck their heads to hide tells.

In Rafe's case, he could be hiding other emotions. If so, he'd been subtle about it. His Stetson added a double dose of hotness and she was susceptible, especially when he added that two-finger salute.

His stack of chips wasn't as big as hers, but close. He'd played carefully all night. His behavior was a one-eighty from the last time she'd faced him across the poker table. Angry and hurt, he'd favored reckless bidding and heavy drinking.

He'd gone easy on the alcohol tonight. Like old times, he'd traded jokes with his brothers and Millie. Not so much with her, but the sulky, resentful guy who'd driven her away from the group two months ago was nowhere to be seen.

The new Rafe glanced at her with a steady gaze and a sense of purpose. Clearly he wanted her to be comfortable here and relaxed in his presence. His top priority was her happiness and the happiness of the people around this table. Noble. Sexy.

Play continued until she and Rafe were the only two left. He'd won the last hand, which brought his winnings almost even with hers.

"I appoint myself the dealer." Jake picked up the cards and began shuffling. "Call it, Rafe."

He met her gaze across the table. "Five-card stud."

Jake kept shuffling. "Wild cards?"

He leaned back in his chair. "Nope."

"Classic choice, bro."

While Jake continued to shuffle, building the suspense, Kate reached in her jeans pocket for her ring. Touching it comforted her and she hadn't been able to stick it in a drawer. Not yet. Maybe the stones had brought her luck. She'd find out when she played poker without it. Maybe next week.

Jake pushed the deck over to her.

She cut the cards. "Good luck, Rafe."

"You, too."

"May the best-looking player win." Jake dealt the first two cards face-down.

"Thanks a lot." Rafe didn't bother looking at his as he nudged back his hat and grinned. "You just jinxed me."

It was the closest he'd come to flirting with her. Instead of checking her hole card, she glanced his way. "Oh, I wouldn't say that."

"I would." Jake dealt her the jack of diamonds face-up. "You're way prettier than this guy." He tilted his head in Rafe's direction and tossed him the king of hearts. "Picture cards all around. Bet 'em like you have 'em."

She peeked at her hole card. The queen of hearts to go with the jack of diamonds. Nice start. Then Jake dealt her another queen. She bet conservatively, slow-playing her hand as she kept an eye on Rafe's.

He got two more hearts to go with his king, but they weren't sequential. Jake dealt her another jack. The gang had been making comments all along, but they went silent as they waited for the last two cards. If her fifth card was a jack or a queen, she'd have a full house.

The best Rafe could do was a flush, assuming he had a heart in the hole. If she didn't get either of those cards and he had that heart, she'd lose. But she'd lose to Rafe, the man she loved. That would be okay. More than okay.

She got another queen, and Jake whistled. "Two pair. Possible full house, lady."

She put on her poker face. "Who knows?"

Rafe got one more heart. Holding her gaze, he shoved his chips to the middle of the table. "All in."

He'd just lost. Her heart squeezed. "Me, too." She shoved her chips forward, mixing them in with his. Then she turned over her queen of hearts.

He turned over his hole card, a club. "Congratulations."

The warmth in his voice and the glow in his dark eyes stole her breath. He'd known he would lose. He could have folded, saved his chips, tried to come back from the loss. Instead he'd surrendered to her.

He pushed away from the table. "Time to pack it in. Get some sleep."

"Yep." Jake was already returning the chips to the holder. "Days are getting shorter. Have to cram more into 'em, now."

Kate stood and picked up a bowl of nuts and another one of chips. "I'll help with—"

"I've got those." Leo took them. "Gather up your winnings, champ."

"I already did that." Rafe came around the table and handed her a cloth bag full of coins and bills. "I'll walk you out."

She blinked in surprise. "Um, sure. Thanks."

"Millie and I will be out in a minute." Jake put the cards in the box with the chips. "I need to check with Garrett to make sure we have everything for Friday night's meal."

"That's fine." She doubted Jake had to check on anything. More likely he was giving Rafe some time alone with her. She walked out of the kitchen. Rafe was by the door, holding her jacket.

Her stomach fluttered. Would that reaction ever go away? Turning her back to him, she slid her arms into the sleeves. He settled the jacket onto her shoulders, his touch light.

She turned. "Thank you. You don't have to—"

"I think I do." He gestured toward the door.

She stepped into the brisk night air and shivered, but not because she was cold. The prospect of a few moments alone with Rafe jacked up her heart rate. He was so... *Rafe*.

He hadn't bothered with a coat. Walking beside her out to Jake's truck, he took a deep breath. "Feels nice out here."

"The pines smell good."

"Yes, ma'am."

She headed for the back door of the cab and faced him. "You were great tonight. I didn't know what to expect, but you were... amazing."

"So were you." He slipped his hands into his pockets. "To be honest, I didn't know if I could do this, but it turns out I can."

"Then you're okay?"

He gave her a crooked smile. "Not yet, but I'll get there. Making progress. Tonight showed me that I might not have everything I want, but at least I'll be able to see you on a regular basis. We'll have times like this. I'm already looking forward to Friday night."

Her throat tightened. "So am I."

"I also wanted to walk you out to prove I can do it without kissing you." He backed away. "Sleep well, Kate."

"You, too, Rafe."

He walked away, his strides purposeful, his back straight. Jake and Millie came out. Jake said something and Rafe laughed.

The sound went straight to her heart and burrowed deep. She missed their intimate meals, their relaxed conversations and their passionate lovemaking. But more than anything else, she missed the joy that filled her soul when Rafe laughed.

33

Rafe had put himself in charge of the fire pit for Friday night's gathering. He'd almost finished arranging logs inside the blackened stones when Nick approached.

"Thanks for the loan of your truck, bro." He handed Rafe the keys. "Can't believe that new fuel pump went bad."

"Glad you could find a replacement so soon." Rafe stood and pocketed the keys.

"Eva followed me back here with the truck. She's inside working on a couple of centerpieces from the leaves she gathered in our yard."

"That'll be festive."

"Yeah, she wanted to add a few touches. The word's out that Wednesday night went well. Everybody's eager for tonight, since you and Kate are solid."

"That's good to hear." Solid? Not yet, but they would be. He'd dedicated all his resources to it. "I'm about ready to light 'er up, if you want to start arranging the chairs."

"I'm on it." He started pulling chairs from the stack and arranging them in a semi-circle around the fire pit while leaving space for dancing.

"Do we have a plan for storing these, yet? We'll have snow before you know it."

"Nobody's using Millie's old room in the cottage." He said it casually, as if talking about Millie's old room was no problem at all. Eventually it wouldn't be. "We could ask Kate if she'd mind shoving them in a corner for the winter. If they're stacked, they won't take up much room."

"She might go for that. At least until Matt gets that storage shed built at his place. He's talked about it but hasn't made it a reality yet."

"He's busy. We're all busy." He wasn't nearly busy enough, but he was working on that, too. He might take up whittling. He finished stuffing newspapers under the logs and struck a match. The dry kindling caught in no time. "I love this fire pit. I can't imagine life without it." He glanced at the time on his phone.

"Got an appointment?"

"I was just looking to see how much longer before Kate will be finished at the dining hall."

"I guess you didn't hear. Henri decided to have Gloria take over on Friday nights so Kate can get here when the rest of us do."

"No kidding?" A jolt of pleasure hit his midsection. "That's great." She could arrive any minute. He was hungry for the sight of her, but he'd play it cool, just like Wednesday night.

"Henri had planned to make the change back in August, but then…"

"We all know what happened then." He added another log to the blaze. "It'll never happen again."

"That's obvious. I'm impressed with how you've handled this. I hear Kate is, too."

"Oh, yeah?" That was happy news. "Bet that came from Millie."

"I think so."

"Is Kate coming over on her own?"

"Matt and Lucy are picking her up." He glanced around. "The ice chest isn't out here yet. I'll get that going." He started toward the bunkhouse and turned around. "Want me to bring you a cold one from the fridge?"

"We're bringing him one," CJ said as he and Isabel came out the back door. "Eva and Millie are stocking the ice chest. Matt and Lucy just pulled up."

"Woo-hoo!" Nick punched a fist in the air. "Time to par-tay!"

"You can say that again." CJ grinned as he approached, his guitar in one hand and his cider in the other. "Beautiful night, isn't it, bro?"

"Definitely."

Isabel glanced at the two bottles she carried and thrust one toward him. "Had to make sure I gave you the alcoholic one."

"Thanks." He'd nurse it the way he had on Wednesday night. Couldn't afford to get toasted until he'd adjusted to this new normal.

She smiled. "I'm so happy to hear that you and Kate are okay."

"I'm happy about it, too."

"Nice fire." CJ settled on a chummy stump and began strumming a few soft chords. "Checked the woodpile on the way out. We need to schedule a lumberjack day soon."

"Yep." Late fall was excellent wood-gathering weather. Last year Kate had made a bunch of pumpkin pies for lumberjack day, adding to the tradition. Thank God they weren't at odds with each other. So many things depended on staying friends.

Nick and Leo came out with the ice chest, a monster the Brotherhood had just bought. When loaded, it took a guy on either end to manage that sucker. But now they had room for enough drinks to last through the evening.

"Stew's almost ready," Leo said. "Can't wait."

Millie and Eva came out behind them, each carrying an arrangement of autumn leaves for the table. Rafe kept glancing at the back door. Kate would walk through any minute now... *there*.

She held a pile of plates topped with napkins and silverware. Matt was carrying a tray of stew bowls and Lucy had two huge baskets of dinner rolls.

The three of them were involved in an animated discussion that absorbed Kate's attention. She flashed Lucy a smile and then turned her head as if searching for... him?

Maybe so. When she made eye contact, her expression brightened. And she blushed. Blushed? Why would she do that? Hadn't happened on Wednesday night.

She walked quickly in his direction. Instead of taking the plates to the table, she came straight to him, her eyes bright, her cheeks still very pink. "Hi."

"Hi, yourself." His heart did a fast two-step. "Can I help you with that?"

She glanced down at the plates, napkins and silverware as if she'd forgotten she had them. "Nope! I've got it." Pivoting, she headed for the table.

He stared after her, confused. "Hey, Matt."

Matt was on his way to the table with his tray loaded with bowls, but he changed direction and came toward the fire pit. "Whatcha need, bro?"

Rafe lowered his voice. "Is Kate okay?"

"She's fine. Why?"

"She... maybe it's my imagination, but she almost looks like she's on something. But I can't believe she'd pop pills to keep her mood up. That's not her style."

Matt smiled. "She's not popping pills. She's just very excited to be here. This is a special night for her. Kind of like a reboot. Starting over."

"Oh." He'd try not to take it personally that she was celebrating the end of their marriage with such joy.

"The fire looks good. Come have some stew. Jake and Garrett are bringing the pots."

"On my way." He added a couple more logs and walked to the long picnic table where folks were jockeying for position, sitting close to make enough room.

The seating was different every time. In a new tradition, couples had decided to split up for chuck wagon stew night. Rafe found a spot between Jake and Leo. Kate was at the far end, miles away.

If Rafe didn't know better, he'd say *everyone* was on something. Chuck wagon stew night was always rambunctious, but tonight the gang was more hyper than they'd been in months.

At one point, Jake stood, which took some doing because he was squashed in, and raised his bottle of cider. "I propose a toast. To Kate and Rafe!"

Damned if everyone didn't join in the toast, lifting their bottles high and shouting *To Kate and Rafe*! He caught her eye to see if she was as bewildered as he was. She didn't look bewildered. And she was still blushing.

CJ finished his meal and returned to the chummy stump. Picking up his guitar, he started playing.

After the first few chords, Rafe turned to stare at him. What the hell? Surely he wouldn't play *I Won't Let Go*. Yep, it seemed he would. This was all a dream. That was the only explanation.

Kate left her seat, walked down to where he sat and held out her hand. Yeah, had to be a dream. Might as well go with it.

He extricated himself from the picnic bench, walked with her to the trampled down area they used for dancing and pulled her into a waltz. "I know this isn't real."

"Actually, it is."

"People in dreams say that all the time."

"It's real." She pinched his earlobe.

"Ow!"

"See?"

"Kate, what the heck is going on?"

She looked up, her gray eyes luminous. "Just dance with me. Please."

"If you say so." He blocked the lyrics at first, but holding her was all he ever wanted to do and eventually he gave himself up to the moment. He'd pay for it later, but for now, for some unknown reason, he was waltzing with the love of his life to the song that had played at the Moose the first time they'd danced, the song that told her all she needed to know.

The music ended. "Thank you for that." His throat ached and his breathing was wonky. "It was nice."

"You're welcome." She stepped back, pulled something from her pocket, and dropped to one knee. "Rafael Stephen Banner, I love you with all my heart. Will you marry me?" She held up his hematite ring.

He gasped. Then he choked. Couldn't breathe…. CJ jumped up, hurried over and whacked him on the back a few times.

Kate scrambled to her feet and clutched his hands, her expression stricken. "Oh, Rafe, I didn't mean to—"

"It's… okay…" His voice was strangled but workable. He could breathe again, sort of. But his brain refused to function. "Just didn't… expect…"

She stepped closer, still clutching his hands. "I love you so much. I've been such an idiot, determined to throw away the best thing in my life, *you*. Wednesday night showed me what I was giving up, who I was giving up. Please say you'll marry me."

"Aren't we…" He cleared his throat. "Already married?"

"Yes, but maybe we should do it again. Let's get *married*. Do you know what I mean?"

Gradually his battered heart opened to her words, to the light in her eyes, the warmth in her voice. "Yes, I do." He swallowed. "Now?"

"Not right now. When we do it, I'd like my mom and sister to be here. In the meantime, will you do me the honor of wearing this?"

"I will." His heart thumped hard as she slid the ring on his finger. "Do you have yours?"

"Right here." She dug in her other pocket. "I can't wait to put it back on."

"Let me." His hand shook, just a little, but he got the ring on.

She gazed up at him. "You may kiss the bride."

With a groan, he pulled her close. As his lips found hers, a deafening racket erupted from the picnic table. Wait. It wasn't just coming from the picnic table. He lifted his head and glanced toward the bunkhouse, where the Babes stood clapping, cheering and whistling. Ben was there, too.

He glanced at Kate as the light dawned. "They all knew you'd be doing this."

"Everybody knew. Except you."

"I'll be damned. That explains a lot." He searched her gaze. "Are we supposed to… is this a party… for us?"

"It is, but nobody expects us to stay."

"Thank God. Let's get out of here." Grabbing her hand, he automatically headed toward the back door. The Babes were in the way. "We're going around." He raised his voice. "Great to see you, ladies. Thanks for the support!" He walked faster, skirting the building.

But as he did, a commotion from the picnic table made him look over his shoulder. They were all up and coming his way. "Hey, we don't need a sendoff! We'll just—"

"Wrong-o!" Jake called out. "You're getting a sendoff whether you want one or not!"

"This is insanity." He made it to the front of the bunkhouse and searched for his truck. Nick had backed in. But that wasn't all he'd done.

Numerous tin cans dangled from the bumper and *Finally Married!!* was painted on his back window, beautifully lettered and embellished with wedding bells, rings and flowers. He started laughing.

"Lucy painted the window and I gathered up a bunch of cans from everybody," Kate said. "I was hoping it would make you laugh."

He looked at her, still grinning. "It's a riot. Great job. I hope the paint lasts a while."

"Lucy said it would unless you want her to take it off."

"I don't. It makes me happy." He paused. "When did you decide?"

"When you walked away Wednesday night. It felt so wrong to have you going in one direction and me in the other."

"Let's not do that anymore."

"Let's not. But I didn't mean to make you choke when I—"

"I love you. You can make me choke any time you want."

"Will you choke if I tell you I want babies?"

"Human babies?"

"Yes! For goodness sakes. Did you think I meant goldfish?"

He smiled. "Just checking."

"You didn't choke."

"No, because I already know you want babies. Let's go home and start making some." He swept her up in his arms and carried her to his truck.

The crowd went wild.

She grinned. "They liked that."

"Then they'll like this even better." He paused by the tailgate and kissed her, long and passionately. Slowly he lifted his head. "That was for the gang, because after all we've put them through, they deserve a show."

She pulled his head down. "And this is for you, because you deserve a lifetime of making love with someone who loves you. Which is me."

He went very still as her lips touched his. She'd kissed him many times in the past week, but never like this. Slowly, tenderly, she pledged her love. At last, her kiss tasted like forever.

New York Times bestselling author Vicki Lewis Thompson's love affair with cowboys started with the Lone Ranger, continued through Maverick, and took a turn south of the border with Zorro. She views cowboys as the Western version of knights in shining armor, rugged men who value honor, honesty and hard work. Fortunately for her, she lives in the Arizona desert, where broad-shouldered, lean-hipped cowboys abound. Blessed with such an abundance of inspiration, she only hopes that she can do them justice.

For more information about this prolific author, visit her website and sign up for her newsletter. She loves connecting with readers.

VickiLewisThompson.com

CPSIA information can be obtained
at www.ICGtesting.com
Printed in the USA
LVHW090019210421
685078LV00017B/417